MOSES:
The Chronicles of Harriet Tubman

BOOK 1: Kings

BOOK 2: Judges

A Novel

By

BALOGUN OJETADE

This is a work of fiction. Any references to real events, persons and locales are intended only to give the fiction a sense of reality and authenticity. All of the characters, organizations and events portrayed in this novel are either products of the author's imagination or used fictitiously.

MOSES:THE CHRONICLES OF HARRIET TUBMAN

Copyright © 2011

All Rights Reserved.

Cover art by Stanley Weaver

Published 2012
Roaring Lions Media, LLC

ISBN-13: 978-1477422885
ISBN-10: 1477422889

To my wife, Iyalogun Ifafunmilayo Ojetade, for her continued support.

To my children – Osunyoyin, Efunsade, Bamitale, Okesina, Yetunde, Abiola, Oluade and Oriyemi – who inspire me to greatness. There is nothing *you cannot achieve!*

To Stanley "Standingo" Weaver, thank you for your Blacknificent cover illustration! Your incomparable work ethic and your amazing talent make you one of the best in the world.

To my fellow Steampunk authors in the League of Extraordinary Black People – Milton J. Davis; Valjeanne Jeffers; and Maurice Broaddus – keep it (Steam)funky! Steamfunk Forever!!

CHAPTER 1

April 10, 1865

Harriet crouched low in the thickets. She counted five – no, *six* – adults in the house. Four men. Two women. They were at the supper table, eating a grayish-brown mass from wooden bowls with their fingers.

A constant, dull thump emanated from the rear of the house.

"Must be the child," Harriet whispered. The girl must be bored, Harriet reasoned, and she was pretending to skip rope, with the heavy chain she was tethered to.

Harriet crept towards the back of the house, but a familiar voice made her pause. She looked skyward.

"I ain't one to question yo' Word, but is you *sure*, Lawd?"

She nodded. "Thy will be done, then."

Harriet stood and brushed the dirt from her dress. She closed her eyes and inhaled deeply. The night air cooled the sweat on her forehead, and the flickering flame in her gut. She opened her eyes and locked her gaze on the house.

In three strong bounds, Harriet was standing at the front door of the house. She pounded her tiny, brown fist on the rotting wood.

The thumping of the heavy chain ceased.

The door was flung open wide.

And the stench of sweat and spoiled milk assaulted her nostrils.

"What you want, gal?"

Harriet quickly peered into the house.

Everyone, except for the wiry man standing before her, was still sitting at the table. But they were no longer eating and their eyes were fixed on the doorway.

The man in the doorway spat onto the porch, the bilious sputum just missing Harriet's boots. "You hear me, nigger? I said…"

The web of flesh between Harriet's thumb and forefinger struck the man's throat. She glided past him as he fell to the floor, clutching his crushed windpipe and gasping for air.

The men at the table jumped to their feet and rushed toward her, as the two women ran toward the rear of the house.

Harriet exploded forward, pummeling the nearest man to her with a flurry of elbow strikes.

Blood erupted from the man's nose and mouth as his face collapsed under the force of Harriet's swift and powerful blows.

Massive arms wrapped around her waist, jerking her into the air.

Harriet threw her head back forcefully. A crunching sound followed and then a scream.

She felt something warm and wet soak the back of her bonnet.

The grip on Harriet's waist loosened slightly. She took advantage of the opportunity, bending forward and grabbing the man-mountain's leg with both hands. Holding on tightly, she rolled forward.

The momentum of the roll forced the giant to tumble over onto his back.

Harriet landed on her back, with the giant's leg between hers. She thrust her hips forward forcefully, ramming her pelvis into the man's knee, as she yanked his ankle back toward her shoulder.

The man-mountain's leg made a loud, popping noise. Harriet tossed the badly twisted leg aside. The giant screamed as his leg flopped around on the floor, no longer under the goliath's control.

Harriet sprang to her feet.

She was met by a powerful punch toward her face as she stood. Harriet shifted slightly to her right and the punch torpedoed past her.

Harriet countered by slamming the heel of her right foot into the man's solar plexus, which sent him careening through the air. He came to rest on the supper table. Slivers of wood and chunks of gray-brown mush sprayed into the air.

The last man turned on his heels and ran toward the door. She kicked an overturned chair. The oak chair flipped through the air and struck the man in the back of the head. The man's head split open like an over-ripe plum. Harriet turned from the dying man and walked to the rear of the house.

The back door was wide open.

The wind had extinguished the candles, but the moon bathed the room in a silver-blue incandescence. The women were – wisely – long gone, but the girl was still in the room, crouched in a corner.

An iron manacle was locked to her right ankle. The manacle was connected to a heavy, iron chain, which was screwed into the floor.

Harriet crouched before the little girl, and placed a gentle hand upon her shoulder. "You alright, baby?"

The little girl perused the room, as if to ensure they were alone, and then nodded.

"You Margaret, I reckon."

The child nodded again.

Harriet rubbed her hand over the girl's matted, light brown curls. "We gon' get you outta here and get you cleaned up. Gotta have you presentable for yo' daddy."

The little girl's eyes widened and the corners of her mouth turned up in the hint of a smile. Yet the act of smiling seemed to strain her, as if she had not smiled in quite some time. "My daddy? He sent you for me?"

Harriet pulled an L-shaped, sliver of metal from behind the ribbon in her bonnet; and slid it into the back of the manacle around Margaret's ankle. "He sure did."

The manacle clicked and slid open.

Margaret caressed her bruised and swollen ankle. “Ma’am, if you don’t mind me asking…”

“Go ‘head, child.”

“Who *are* you?” Margaret asked.

Harriet stood, and helped the little girl to her feet. “Me? I’m Harriet. Harriet Tubman.”

CHAPTER 2

April 8, 1865

Booth unbuttoned his topcoat and removed a small, neatly folded piece of paper from his vest. He looked down at the paper, and then up at the large, two-story brick house that stood before him.

"One-eighty, South Street. Here we are!"

Booth sauntered up the walkway. Halfway to the front door, the welcoming smell of hot biscuits met him. Booth's mouth watered. He swallowed and then moistened his lips with his tongue.

He stood at the door and raised his hand to knock. But the door opened before his fist could make contact with it.

"Good mornin', suh. How may I help you?"

Booth looked down at the tiny woman in the doorway. Her eyes were studying his. He took off his derby, placed it over his heart and bowed slightly.

"Good morning! Harriet Tubman, I presume?"

Harriet nodded. "Yes, suh."

"My name is John Wilkes Booth, and I am in dire need of your assistance," he said.

"*My* assistance?"

Booth leaned closer to Harriet. His eyes darted from side to side as if he was about to share some great secret.

"The kind of assistance only someone who possesses your skills can provide."

Harriet nodded. "Come on in and let's talk." She turned and walked towards the kitchen. Booth followed.

"You hungry," She asked. "I'm cooking breakfast for my mama and daddy, but there's plenty."

"I'm famished," Booth replied.

Harriet gestured toward the table. "Then, take a seat, please, and I'll be right with you."

Booth sat down, placing his derby in his lap. He watched Harriet as she carried a tray of food upstairs.

He smiled. It amused him that such a renowned, and even feared soldier and spy as "General" Tubman, would be doing domestic work.

Niggras are such an enigma! He chuckled at the rhyme. *I must remember that, for use forth*coming!

Harriet returned to the kitchen and prepared two plates. She handed one to Booth, and sat across from him at the table.

He brought the plate up to his nose and inhaled. "Mmm…grits, eggs and venison sausage. Good eating!"

She nodded. "Yes, suh."

As Booth sated his hunger, Harriet studied him. There was something familiar about the man, but she couldn't discern what.

Booth tossed the final piece of sausage into his mouth, and closed his eyes as he chewed; enjoying the spicy-sweet, smoked flavor. He swallowed and drew a handkerchief from his vest pocket, flicking it open dramatically.

He dabbed at the corners of his mouth. "That was delicious, Harriet...delicious, indeed."

"Thank you, suh," Harriet replied as she pushed her half-eaten plate to the side. "Not trying to be unkind, Mr. Booth, but I'm sure it ain't my cookin' skills you in need of."

"You are absolutely right, Harriet," Booth said. "I am here to beg for your help and to pay you, in kind, for said assistance."

"And what is it that you need me to do, Mr. Booth?" Harriet asked.

"Before the war, I spent much of my time in the company of a gal, who was the property of a friend of mine in Cambridge, Maryland – a place with which you are quite familiar, I am told."

Harriet nodded. “Yes, suh. Born and raised up the road from there, in Bucktown.”

“Well, that gal bore me a child…Margaret,” Booth said. “She's eight years old. The prettiest little lady you could ever lay eyes upon.”

Booth rapped his fingers on the supper table, beating a quick, staccato rhythm. “Recently, I was forced to flee Maryland and to leave my beloved Margaret alone, in the care of her mama.”

“And now, somethin’ has happened,” Harriet said. “Somethin’ *bad*, if you comin’ to me for help.”

“Yes,” Booth replied. “I recently received word that Margaret’s mother was killed; and my baby girl is being held captive by a family of miscreants in Cambridge.”

Booth leaned forward in his chair and rested his forearms on the supper table. “They are demanding twelve thousand dollars for her return.”

“Lawd...” Harriet breathed.

“I tried to get the money,” Booth said, “God knows I did. But I was only able to come up with five thousand. They will kill my Margaret if I do not pay them, in full, by the eleventh of this month.”

“And you want me to bring yo’ little girl back to you.”

He nodded. “I’ll pay you the five thousand dollars I raised up front, plus your transport to – and from – Cambridge.”

Harriet rose from her chair and extended her right hand. Booth smiled and took her hand in his. She shook his hand briskly. “Reckon I best get goin.’ Yo’ little girl is waitin’ to come home.”

CHAPTER 3

April 12, 1865

Harriet and Margaret held each others' hands as they walked toward Harriet's house. Margaret pointed at the elderly black man and woman who sat in rocking chairs on the porch. "Who is that?"

"That's my mama and daddy," Harriet replied. "Miss. Rit and Mr. Ben."

The little girl looked around her. She stood on her tip-toes and craned her neck. "Where is my daddy?" she asked.

"I don't rightly know, child," Harriet replied. "Maybe he inside."

As they drew close to the house, Harriet called out. "Hey, mama! Hey, Daddy!"

Her parents waved. Ben squinted as he stared at Margaret. "Who child is dat?"

"Her name is Margaret, daddy," Harriet replied. "She Mr. Booth's child."

Margaret snatched away from Harriet, her face a mask of confusion and fright.

"Who is Mr. Booth?" Margaret cried. "Booth is *not* my daddy's name! My daddy's name is *Stanton. Edwin* Stanton!"

Harriet placed her leathery hand on the child's shoulder. "Secretary of *War*, Edwin Stanton?"

"Yes...!"

Harriet shook her hand, and looked skyward. "Lawd, show me the way."

The morning sky had grown dark and the wind, very, very cold.

CHAPTER 4

April 13, 1865

Booth removed his derby, as he entered the capacious office. "John Wilkes Booth at your service."

Secretary of War Edwin M. Stanton took a long drag on his cigar, and then blew a ring of smoke out of the window. "Close the door."

Booth closed the door behind him, and moved towards the chairs that sat before Stanton's desk.

"I did *not* offer you a chair!" Stanton barked.

Booth stopped in his tracks and then took two steps backward. "Apologies."

"You said you have information in regard to my daughter's whereabouts?"

Booth smiled slyly. "I do…and more."

Stanton took another drag of his cigar, and again blew smoke-rings out the window, which he continued to stare out of. "Speak, sir, or life for you will swiftly take a turn for the worse."

Booth's smile grew into a wide grin. He fanned himself with his derby. The light breeze he generated made his curly hair roll in gentle waves across his head. "It truly is a new day when a niggra can talk so strongly to a white man!"

The cigar cradled between Stanton's fingers quivered. He swallowed hard. "What…what did you say?"

"Oh, yes," Booth hopped into a chair and threw his feet up onto the mahogany desk. "I know all about you. You have them all fooled. Even your wife. When she looks at Margaret, though, she *has* to wonder."

Stanton leaned forward, bringing his face within an inch of Booth's. "If you know all about me, then you know about my special…gifts." He brought his cigar to his lips.

"Do it," Booth shot back, "and you will *never* see your daughter again."

Stanton stared at him a moment, and then sat back in his chair. "What do you want?" He sighed.

"I want access," Booth replied.

"Access?"

"Yes. I keep your little…black secret *and* I tell you the whereabouts of your daughter; in exchange for access to President Abraham Lincoln."

"When?"

"Tomorrow evening…at the Ford Theater."

CHAPTER 5

April 14, 1865

The Ford Theater was energized by the resounding laughter that filled its voluminous house and narrow hallways. *Our American Cousin* was a smashing success, and a play that Booth knew well. He had turned down the lead role of Asa Trenchard just a few months ago.

Booth loved a good comedy. But *Our American Cousin* was beneath a renowned Shakespearean actor such as himself.

He smiled. *Tonight will be my greatest performance. But certainly not my last.* The thespian walked up the narrow stairway to the Presidential box.

At the zenith, there was no guard on post; just as Stanton had promised.

Booth peeked into the box. His target was holding Mary Todd Lincoln's hand. Every so often, Mrs. Lincoln would share a loving glance with her husband.

His heart soared, at the thought of Abraham Lincoln's brains soiling Mary Todd's pretty, new dress.

Sharing the box with the Lincolns was Major Henry Rathbone – an easy enough kill, if need be – and his fiancée, Clara Harris.

Booth inhaled deeply, closed his eyes and listened.

Harry Hawk was in rare form tonight, in the lead role of Asa. The audience was eating out of the palm of his hand, and their palates were well-rewarded.

"Don't know the members of good society, eh...?" Harry Hawk began.

Booth withdrew a small, Philadelphia Derringer pistol from the inner pocket of his topcoat.

Harry Hawk continued to deliver his lines. "*Well, I guess I know enough to turn you inside out, old gal; you sockdologizing old man-trap!*"

The theater erupted in laughter. Booth rushed into the Presidential box, and pointed his tiny pistol at the back of Lincoln's head. The gun's oak grip felt uncharacteristically warm in Booth's palm.

He quickly inhaled, drawing in a wisp of breath and then squeezed the trigger.

Lincoln's head snapped forward.

A torrent of blood, bone and brain rained from where the President's face once was.

Mrs. Lincoln screamed as a piece of her husband's skull landed in her lap.

Clara Harris fell to the floor, screaming – as Major Rathbone leaped from his chair and ran towards Booth.

Booth tossed his spent pistol to the floor, and then drew his knife from the sheath on his belt. Major Rathbone reached out and caught Booth's lapel in a powerful grip. Booth slashed viciously with his knife-wielding hand.

The sleeve of Major Rathbone's Union blue topcoat turned black, as blood poured from the wide gash in his upper arm. The young Major stumbled backward, clutching his arm in pain.

Booth ran to the railing and climbed it.

Major Rathbone shook his head furiously, as if to expel the pain and fear from his brain and out of his ears. He lurched forward, reaching out toward Booth the assailant as he ran to the balcony's railing.

Booth slashed at Major Rathbone's face with the point of his knife.

Major Rathbone quickly back-pedaled – tapping his face with his fingers to ensure no damage was done.

Booth leaped from the scene of his grisly handiwork, landing on the stage far below. His left ankle shattered upon impact. He fell to the floor in pain, but, driven by madness, quickly pulled himself to his feet.

Booth looked out at the cringing audience, raised his knife far above his head and shouted: "Sic semper tyrannis!"

Thus always to tyrants.

The iron-fisted "king" of the Union was dead. It was now time for Booth to begin the second act of his play.

He quickly hobbled off the stage, shambled out the door, hopped onto his horse and rode off into the night.

CHAPTER 6

April 15, 1865

"That's right! Shot him dead! On Good Friday, no less!"

Harriet liked old 'Pop' Alexander. He could read as good as most white folks, and he loved to deliver the news – good and bad.

Harriet reached for the newspaper that sat upon Pop's lap. "And you sure it was Mr. Booth?"

Pop opened the paper and read the headline: "Famed actor, John Wilkes Booth, assassinates President Lincoln." He turned the front page toward Harriet.

She studied the photograph under the headline. The curly hair; the trimmed mustache; the smug expression. It was, most certainly, John Wilkes Booth – the same Booth who'd paid her a huge sum of money to save a little girl he claimed was his child.

But the child had never laid eyes upon him and was, in fact, the daughter of the Secretary of War.

"Lawd," Harriet sighed, shaking her head.

She bent her knees a bit, and picked up a small burlap sack that lay at her feet. "Here's some fresh biscuits for you, Pop."

Pop took the sack from her, opened the bag and sniffed. His lips stretched upwards into a smile. "Keep it up and I'm gon' have to marry you!"

Harriet laughed. "Don't say it, 'less you mean it." She waved her hands high above her head. "Thank you Pop. Gon' go home and pray on all this. I'll come by and see you in a week or so."

"You're welcome, Harriet," Pop replied. "Godspeed!"

She turned and began walking up the road, then stopped and looked up at the clear, early morning sky. "I don't know much, Lawd, but I *do* know that you are the way, the truth and the light.

Please, show me what it all means, Lawd – Booth, Margaret, President Lincoln's death and Secretary of War, Edwin Stanton."

Harriet lowered her gaze and then picked up her pace. "I know trouble's comin,' Father. Please protect me from it, and prepare me for it when it arrives, Lawd. Amen."

CHAPTER 7

April 17, 1865

"Margaret," Harriet called.

There was no answer.

"Margaret: come eat, child!"

Harriet was answered with a barely audible sob. She followed the sound to the back of the house. "Margaret?"

Harriet opened the back door and stepped outside. She found the little girl sitting against the rear wall. Her arms were wrapped around her shins and her forehead rested upon her bent knees. Margaret's tiny frame shook as she wept.

She hopped off the porch, and sat down on a patch of grass next to Margaret."What's all the fuss about, child?"

The child raised her head and stared at Harriet. Her olive-toned cheeks were wet with tears. "You said my daddy would be here! I want my daddy! I want my mommy!"

Harriet ran her small, but strong fingers through Margaret's thick curls. "Your Auntie Harriet always make good on her promises, child. You'll see yo' daddy soon. Yo' mama too."

"H–how soon?" Margaret asked.

"The Lawd say he gon' show me the way real soon. When He give it to me, I'll let you know, alright?

"Alright."

Harriet stood up and then extended her hand toward Margaret. "Now, come on, let's go eat."

CHAPTER 8

April 23, 1865

The graveyard gate was locked.

Harriet gracefully bounded halfway to the top of the tall, iron barrier and climbed the rest of the way to the apex.

She looked around, examining the grounds. The graveyard was still and quiet.

She leaped down into the cemetery. The moist ground sank slightly beneath her boots. A rank odor rose from under her feet – the smell of withered moss, rotting wood and possum.

Harriet crouched low and scuttled across the graveyard like a crab, until she came to a large, onyx tombstone. Upon the stone was chiseled, simply: *John B.*

"Booth," Harriet whispered.

She drew her Colt Army Model 1860 revolver from its worn, leather holster; aimed it at the soft ground in front of the onyx tombstone and fired all six rounds into the dirt.

Blood began to spray up from each bullet hole and form a puddle in front of the tombstone.

A fist punched through the blood and dirt.

Shocked, Harriet stumbled backward and fell.

Another hand reached up through the puddle of ichor.

The hands sank their fingers into the blood-soaked earth; and then, with a forceful pull, freed the rest of their body from its bloody grave. The body was that of a wiry man.

Harriet strained to see the man's face through the blood, filth and darkness upon his visage.

He growled and leaped at her like a feral dog. She tried to roll to safety, but her arms and legs were – strangely – too heavy to move.

The feral man snatched Harriet into the air and tossed her over its broad shoulder.

Suddenly, the world seemed to shift…to transmogrify.

Harriet found herself at the gallows, with a noose around her neck. She could feel his breath on the back of her neck. The noose grew tighter…and tighter…and…

CHAPTER 9

April 23, 1865

"Aunt Harriet? *Aunt Harriet?!"*

Margaret shook Harriet's muscular shoulders. Harriet slumped down in her chair. A line of spittle fell from her lips, and dripped onto the toe of her boot.

Margaret shook her more forcefully. "Aunt Harriet! Wake up!"

"*Hush, child!*"

She turned toward the strong alto voice. The voice belonged to Mama Rit.

"Mama, something's wrong with Aunt Harriet," Margaret began. "We were talking and she just fell asleep! I don't..."

Mama Rit raised her hand. The little girl fell silent.

Harriet's mother pulled her back up in her chair. "Harriet been havin' these spells, ever since a old overseer hit her in the head wit' a big ol' piece o' iron when she was twelve years ol'."

"That's terrible," Margaret said, shaking her little head.

"Not *too* terrible," Mama Rit replied. "When she get them spells, the Lawd speak to her an' show her all kinds o' mysteries."

Harriet awoke with a start. She ran her fingers over her neck and breathed a sigh of relief when she found no noose there.

Margaret wrapped her little arms around Harriet's chest and squeezed. "Aunt Harriet! Thank God you woke up!"

"I always do, child," Harriet replied. "We gotta get ready. We gon' be leavin' here soon, child. The Lawd gon' show me where in a day or two."

"Leaving?" Margaret asked. "Why?

"Death comin.' We don't wanna greet him 'round here."

"Mama Rit and Papa Ben are leaving too?"

"No, child. Just you and me," Harriet answered. "Death don't want them just yet. And I don't want Him to come here, and make their acquaintance either."

A chill ran up the little girl's back and nipped at her ears. She shivered. "So, Death is after *us*?"

"*I'm* the one He fishin' fo.' You just the critter on the line."

CHAPTER 10

April 24, 1865

Harriet stood in her doorway, enjoying the cool, morning air and the quiet company of her parents.

Mama Rit divided her attention between a squirrel, which leaped from limb to limb of an old, oak tree, and Margaret, who was gleefully chasing the neighbor's mutt puppy around the front yard. Papa Ben's concentration was on the piece of wood in his hands, which he carved with precision and patience.

"What you makin,' daddy?" Harriet asked.

Papa Ben continued to adroitly carve the wood. "I'm makin' an angel for yo' Mama."

"*An angel, for an angel*," a voice said from the side of the house.

Harriet and her parents turned their gaze towards the voice.

A young man, in his mid-teens, came around the corner of the house.

Although, when she last saw him he was just a boy, Harriet recognized him immediately. "Ben!"

The young man ran to the porch with his arms outstretched. "Auntie Harriet!"

Harriet and Ben embraced for a long while; and then he turned to Mama Rit and kissed her on the cheek.

"Grandma Rit! How you doin'?"

Mama Rit grabbed Ben's hands and studied his face with her loving eyes. "Better, now that you here."

"How yo' daddy and yo' mama?" Papa Ben asked.

The younger Ben kissed the elder Ben on the forehead. "They fine, last I seen 'em... Been a while, though."

"Been a while?" Papa Ben inquired.

"Yes, suh. Been travelin' around, workin' here and there."

Harriet smiled. Her nephew had grown to be strong and responsible. "You hungry, boy?"

"I'm *famished*!" Ben replied.

Harriet was chilled by Ben's words. Booth had spoken them just over two weeks ago. "Gon' in the kitchen," Harriet said. "There's bacon and biscuits. I'll come fix you some grits and eggs shortly."

He smiled. "Thank you, auntie." The young man scooted past Harriet, into the house, and followed his nose to the kitchen.

Harriet looked skyward and shook her head. "Signs, upon signs. Please, close my eyes, Lawd, so that I might see."

CHAPTER 11

April 26, 1865

Secretary of War, Edwin M. Stanton hated the time just before dawn. The air was too damp, too cold. This was the time when slaves began their work, in the brutal fields of tobacco, cotton and cane.

This was the time that reminded him most of his beloved, adopted mother, toiling in those fields; until exposure to the damnable pre-dawn air took her from him.

Stanton spat into the air, as if to defile it. A sudden movement in the distant darkness caught his eye. Stanton's hand crept toward the Colt Dragoon revolver in the cross-draw holster on his hip. "Show yourself!"

A man in Union blue stepped out of the shadows – along with another young man who was dressed in civilian clothes. As the men drew closer, Stanton recognized the civilian's curly hair, thick, neatly trimmed mustache and smug expression.

"Booth...!" he whispered.

"No, not quite," the young man replied. "I am not John Wilkes Booth, sir. I am just his friend and fellow thespian, Lafayette Downs." The Booth doppelganger bowed dramatically. "But with the right stage make-up and costuming, an actor such as I can become anyone."

Stanton shook Downs' hand, and looked toward the Union officer accompanying him. The officer snapped to attention and crisply brought his fingertips to his brow in salutation. Stanton returned the salute. "Lieutenant Colonel..."

"Sir!"

Lieutenant Colonel Conger, Intelligence Officer, was the most ruthless and efficient soldier Stanton had ever met. Stanton liked him. He didn't mind getting bloody.

The Secretary of War turned his attention to Downs. "What news do you bring me?"

"John sends his warmest regards," Downs replied. "He wanted to let you know that your daughter is doing quite well. She is in the care of your dear friend, Harriet Tubman, at her home in Auburn, New York."

Stanton frowned. "Harriet Tubman? *The* Harriet Tubman?"

"That is correct."

Stanton extended his hand toward Downs. The young man grabbed Stanton's hand and shook it. "Thank you, Mr. Downs. Tell Booth it was a brilliant idea to have you come looking like him, so we would know that he really sent the message."

"I most certainly shall," Downs replied.

Stanton released his hand. "Thank you, again. Colonel Conger, see Mr. Downs on his way."

"Sir," Lieutenant Colonel Conger said.

Colonel Conger swiftly drew his revolver, aimed and fired.

The bullet struck Downs in the back of the neck. The actor collapsed. His body lay still. But his eyes remained open, looking to and fro, as if he was trying to assess his whereabouts. He opened his mouth to speak, yet his vocal chords – like the rest of him – were paralyzed.

Stanton examined Downs' body and nodded in approval. "Good work. We have our Booth. Now, do we have the man who killed him?"

"Yes, sir," Colonel Conger replied. "Sergeant Boston Corbett. Quite insane."

"Excellent! Set it up!"

Stanton pulled a cigar from the inner pocket of his topcoat. He bit the tip of it, lit it and took a quick puff. He turned from Colonel Conger, and blew the smoke into the pre-dawn air he so despised. “If you need me, I will be at home: planning my trip to Auburn, New York.”

CHAPTER 12

April 26, 1865

The thick log split easily under the force of Harriet's axe. She swung the tool with superb skill and tremendous strength; cleaving log after log as leisurely, as a chef slicing ripe tomatoes.

Ben slammed his axe into an old tree stump. "Auntie Harriet?"

Harriet stopped chopping, and tossed her axe onto her shoulder. The heavy tool made a dull thud as it landed on the dense muscles of her shoulder and chest. She turned from the wood pile, and wiped the sweat from her brow. "Yes, boy?"

"Margaret say, y'all leaving Auburn."

Harriet nodded. "We are. Soon as the Lawd say when."

"Well, way I see it," Ben began. "You gon' need help. Somebody you can trust to help you with the care of that little girl, 'til she safe with her family."

Harriet smiled. "And that be *you*, I imagine."

"Yes, ma'am."

"Well, when we…"

The words were suddenly like anvils on her tongue.

The world narrowed and elongated. Tilted. Whirled.

Harriet closed her eyes and fought back a wave of nausea.

A sudden, terrible constriction of her throat forced Harriet's eyes open. The world swayed back and forth; side to side. Harriet realized it was not actually the world swaying…it was her, swinging and swaying from the end of a noose.

The pressure on Harriet's throat tightened.

Through her pain and encroaching light-headedness, she recognized movement in her peripheral vision. Something *huge*.

A steam locomotive slowly rode past Harriet. She spotted the engineer – an elderly Mexican woman who wore nothing, save an oversized sombrero upon her small head.

Harriet's vision began to fade, yet her gaze remained locked on the engineer.

The engineer.

The engine…

Blackness.

Light.

Harriet squinted as sunlight bathed her irises.

"Auntie Harriet, are you alright?" Ben cradled Harriet's head in his arms as he rocked back and forth.

Harriet looked into Ben's eyes, using his face as confirmation she had returned from the dreaming. "Gather your things, boy! We goin' to Mexico!"

CHAPTER 13

April 26, 1865

The Oxblood Inn – called, simply, *The Oxblood*, by its many regular patrons – was uncharacteristically quiet.

Edwin Stanton had used gold from the military coffers to rent the saloon for the rest of the night. The Secretary of War sat at the bar with the owner of *The Oxblood,* Mr. Enthwhistle: a quintessential English Gentleman.

"You cannot be serious," Stanton said, shaking his head. "There is nothing about a pipe that satisfies like a good cigar."

"Are you mad?" Mr. Enthwhistle disappeared from sight. A moment later, he reappeared, flipping a mahogany pipe between his well-manicured fingers. "This – my good man – is a bloody work of art!"

Stanton reached for the pipe. "Let me see that delicate little thing!"

Mr. Enthwhistle disappeared from view and – almost instantaneously – reappeared behind Stanton. "Afraid *not*, mate. This churchwarden has been in me family for over a century. *No one* touches her but me!"

The English gent disappeared again and quickly reappeared. The pipe was gone. It had been replaced by an ivory walking stick. The handle of the cane was a pearl the size of a man's fist. "When do our esteemed guests arrive?"

"They should be here any minute now," Stanton replied.

"I have never encountered the…others," Mr. Enthwhistle said. "I look forward to this meeting."

"You might soon change your mind, comrade," said a sultry voice.

Mr. Enthwhistle turned toward the entrance. Standing before him was a sight he had seen just once, while in Dahomey, West Africa: a woman in trousers. "And you are?"

"Druga Minkoff," the woman answered, as she sauntered to the bar.

Mr. Enthwhistle appeared behind the well-polished, red oak bar. He held out a shot glass and a bottle of clear liquid toward Druga. "Vodka, my Czaritsa?"

"I am no queen," Druga answered. "However, no good Russian would *ever* refuse vodka."

Druga smiled.

Mr. Enthwhistle was captivated by her teeth, which were more canine than human and about an inch larger than normal. He handed Druga her glass, and filled it.

Two men walked into the saloon. To Mr. Enthwhistle, they were indistinguishable from each other; except one wore a brown wool gambler hat, and the other sported a black coachman hat.

"The Twin cowboys," Mr. Enthwhistle breathed.

"That's right," the twin in the coachman hat replied. His words lingered on his tongue. "My name's Caleb Butler and this here's my brother, Donald."

Donald nodded his head as he tipped the brim of his hat. "Yup."

Stanton raised a shot glass toward the twins. "Gentlemen, good to see you! I was not sure you'd come."

"Why?" Caleb asked. "Because of y'all's li'l Civil War?"

"Of course," Stanton answered.

"Look, me and Donald don't give a damn about no Confederate gray or Union blue."

"Nope," Donald chimed in.

Caleb briskly rubbed his forefinger and middle finger against his thumb. "We care about gold and silver."

"Yup," Donald replied.

"So, gents," Mr. Enthwhistle began. "What can I get you to…"

A man's scream gave pause to Mr. Enthwhistle's words.

Stanton leaped off of his stool and darted toward the door. "Damn it! Mama Maybelle!"

"It's okay, baby!" a powerful voice bellowed from just outside the entrance to *The Oxblood.*

A mountainous woman stepped into view. Her stark-white smile – accentuated by her cocoa skin – beamed brightly. The woman stooped to clear the top of the doorway and shuffled in sideways. "Me and some folk 'round here just had a misunderstandin' is all."

"I reckon so," Caleb said. "A giant, niggra gal enterin' a white man's establishment might be a bit upsettin' to some. You lucky to be alive!"

Mama Maybelle shook her head. "Child, I been *alive* since before your great grandmammy spat your grandmammy out of her hole. And I'm gon' be the last one standin' come the Day of Judgment – all 'cause o' *these*." Mama Maybelle held up her massive fists. They were caked in blood.

"How many dead, Maybelle?" Stanton sighed.

"'Bout fifteen…sixteen, child. Maybe more."

Stanton approached Maybelle. Although he was a tall bear of a man himself, next to Mama Maybelle, he looked infantile. "Okay, I'll have my men clean it up. Now let's get down to business!"

Stanton grabbed a stack of papers from the bar and handed a page to each of the guests. Harriet's battle-hardened visage greeted them. "*She* is your target, ladies and gentlemen. Harriet Tubman, also known as Araminta Ross and Moses."

Caleb shook his head and nudged his brother in the ribs. "Sure don't look like much, does she?"

"Nope," Donald answered.

"Do not be fooled," Stanton warned. "Harriet Tubman is unique – like us – but with more experience using her gifts than all of us combined…excluding Mama Maybelle, of course."

"Course, child," Mama Maybelle said with a nod.

"As the Secretary of War – and as one of the gifted myself – I have been in charge of identifying, recruiting and utilizing every known gifted in this great nation of ours," Stanton said. "However, Harriet has been allowed to operate with total autonomy; and has refused to have the limits of her gifts examined. She claims that her powers come from God, and are not for man to have full knowledge of."

Stanton handed everyone another piece of paper, upon which was a picture of Margaret. "For reasons unknown to me, Harriet has spirited away my daughter, Margaret. She's holding her captive in Auburn, New York."

Tears welled in Stanton's eyes and his gruff voice grew soft. "Margaret is eight years old. She is a bit small for her age. Sweet as potato pie. I want her back, unharmed! Twenty thousand dollars to the man or woman who succeeds in this."

"And, Harriet Tubman?" Mr. Enthwhistle inquired.

"Ten thousand dollars for her heart," Stanton replied. "Twenty thousand dollars for her *head*!"

CHAPTER 14

April 27, 1865

"Margaret! Come on down, child! The coach is here!"

Harriet stood in the doorway, rapping her fingers on the smooth, wooden back of her mother's rocking chair. Papa Ben and Mama Rit sat in their chairs, rocking slowly and bathing in the waves of cool morning air.

Papa Ben's namesake, the younger Ben, tossed the bags onto the top of the coach; and then tethered them with a thick length of rope.

Mama Rit gently tugged at Harriet's arm. "Where y'all say y'all was headed to, again?"

"To Galveston, Texas, mama," Harriet replied.

Mama Rit and Papa Ben exchanged quick glances.

"Galveston, Texas it *is*, then," Papa Ben said as he winked at Mama Rit.

Harriet hated to lie, especially to her parents, who always knew when she wasn't being truthful with them.

"Daddy, I…" Harriet began.

"Baby, we know you got yo' reasons fo' not tellin' us the whole truth," Papa Ben said, interrupting her. "And yo' reasons always been good ones, far as we can tell. So, just take care of yo' self and them beautiful children."

"And come home, soon," Mama Rit added.

"I will, y'all. I will," Harriet replied.

Harriet kissed her parents, and then dodged out of the way as Margaret skipped past her.

"Bye, Mama Rit…Papa Ben!" Margaret shouted as she bounded down the stairs.

Harriet followed her off the porch and to the coach.

Ben hoisted Margaret into the coach's carriage. The child pounced into the seat inside, bouncing up and down on its springy cushion. The leather cooled her skin. She sat still for a moment, enjoying its calming touch, before resuming her bouncing. "Come on, Ben! Come on!"

"On my way, little mouse!" Ben climbed into the carriage and took a seat next to Margaret.

"You ever sit next to a white person in a carriage before, Ben?" Margaret asked.

"Can't say I has," Ben replied.

"Is it fun?" The little girl inquired.

"Can't say. I ain't never sat by one."

Margaret's brow furrowed, and she stared at Ben with a confused expression. "What do you mean, Ben? *I'm* white!"

"No, you ain't. You just high, *high* yella, is all."

"I *am* white! My mommy is white, my *daddy* is white…so how can I be…"

Harriet leaped into the carriage and closed the door. "Some things is better left fo' yo' *folks* to explain," she said, as she glared at Ben.

Ben and Margaret both stared at the floor and replied in unison. "Yes, ma'am."

The coach departed. Harriet waved farewell to her parents.

"Auntie Harriet," Ben said, tapping her on the knee. "I didn't know any trains went from here all the way to Texas.

"There's a lot we don't know 'bout this world," Harriet said solemnly, "even though it's right befo' our eyes, under our feet or above our heads."

"What you mean by that, Auntie?"

"You'll see soon enough, boy. You'll see."

CHAPTER 15

April 27, 1865

Druga stepped off the train and sniffed the air. Every city in America had a distinct smell. Auburn, New York smelled of lake water, iron and corn.

She extended her hand toward Stanton, who stood at her right flank. "The cloth, please."

Stanton pulled a small, white dress from his bag and handed it to Druga. "She wore this the day before she went missing," Stanton said.

Druga sniffed the cloth. She shook her head and handed it back to Stanton. "Your daughter has not been anywhere near this station."

"Good," Stanton replied. "The waterways only cover this county, so they would not use them. The next train doesn't leave until tomorrow morning."

"So there is a good chance they are still here," said Mr. Enthwhistle.

"A *great* chance," Stanton replied. "Let's depart quickly to Harriet's home! God blesses the swift!"

CHAPTER 16

April 27, 1865

Papa Ben gazed heavenward. The sky was clear, but the air and the earth rumbled with distant thunder.

"Ben...!" Mama Rit cried.

Papa Ben turned his attention to Mama Rit, who was pointing at the horizon.

Several people rode upon horses toward them – and they were riding hard.

Papa Ben jumped from his chair. "Rit, get in the house!"

The elderly couple hastened into the house and secured the doors. They then sat quietly in the kitchen in shadow...far from the windows.

* * *

Stanton and his hunters rode up to Harriet's house, and dismounted from their horses. Mama Maybelle stepped down from her coach.

Druga sniffed the air. "Your daughter is not here. She was, but not anymore. Her scent leads further up the road."

Stanton spat upon the grass. "Damn it!"

Druga sniffed the air again. "All is not lost. There are two people inside of the house."

"Harriet!" Stanton growled.

"I do not think so, tovarisch," Druga replied. "They smell…old."

"Mr. Enthwhistle," Stanton began. "If you would be so kind as to…"

The front door of Harriet's house opened slowly. Caleb swiftly drew his revolvers. Donald raised his rifle and aimed it at the doorway.

Mr. Enthwhistle stepped through the doorway from the inside of Harriet's house. "There are two aged blacks inside. I have rendered them both unconscious. Please, come in."

"Nice trick," Caleb said.

"Yup," Donald agreed.

The band of hunters followed Mr. Enthwhistle into Harriet's kitchen.

Papa Ben and Mama Rit were both lying on the floor. A knot the size of a marble had grown on Papa Ben's forehead.

"Pick them up, please," Stanton said.

Mama Maybelle snatched up Mama Rit and Papa Ben, as if she was plucking apples from a barrel. She tossed them into chairs at the supper table. The resulting jolt awakened them.

Stanton sat between the couple. He drew his revolver from its holster, and gently placed it on the kitchen table. "Please, forgive us for this intrusion. We will not tarry long."

He rested his hand on his revolver and smiled. "I am Secretary of War, Edwin Stanton. I presume you are Ms. Harriet Tubman's parents?"

Papa Ben nodded.

"Good," Stanton said. "Then you can tell us where she is. Where *is* Ms. Tubman?"

"Don't rightly know," Papa Ben answered. "When I woke up, she was gone. She *do* that."

Druga sniffed the air. "He stinks of a lie!"

Stanton leaped to his feet, snatching the gun from the table at lightning speed. He pressed the barrel against Mama Rit's neck. "Time is of the essence, sir! Tell me where Harriet is right *now*, or I will separate your wife's head from her shoulders!"

"Alright, suh!" Papa Ben screamed. "Alright! She left for Galveston, Texas this morning!"

Stanton looked at Druga. "Well?"

Druga nodded. "He is telling the truth."

Caleb exchanged glances with his brother. "Excuse me, but we are from Houston. I can assure, you that no train travels *that* far south from the North."

"Nope," Donald agreed.

Stanton tugged at his beard. "There is *one*."

Caleb tilted his head and squinted at Stanton. "Huh?"

The Secretary of War trotted toward the front door. He turned to face the hunters, "Water your horses and saddle up! We are riding back to Washington!"

CHAPTER 17

April 27, 1865

The night air in Philadelphia sent a chill through the coach. Margaret snuggled closer to Ben.

"Are we riding this coach all the way to Mexico, Auntie?" Ben asked.

"What's the matter? It's not comfortable enough for you?" Harriet replied.

"It's *very* comfortable, Auntie. But it is powerful cold out, and a trip that far might take us a week or more." Ben rubbed the little girl's shoulders with his palms. "Why, Margaret be froze solid by then!"

The coach came to a gentle halt. The coach driver – a stout little man with ebony skin – was nearly invisible in the dull glow of the moon, as he approached the door of the coach.

"Margaret…Ben," Harriet whispered. "What you 'bout to see and do, ain't fo' you to speak of to just anybody. You understand me?"

Margaret nodded.

Ben peered out of the carriage window. He could make out a small, domed building in the middle of a vast field of wheat. Nothing special. "I guess so, Auntie."

The coach driver opened the door. "Leave your bags," the man said. His voice was deep, rich; with just a hint of a West African accent. "My apprentice will gather them. Come now... Quietly."

Harriet climbed out of the coach and Margaret and Ben followed. The little girl clutched Harriet's hand tightly, as they followed the coach driver down a dark trail through the wheat field...toward the domed building in the distance.

As they drew closer to the structure – which was surrounded by torches, whose flames licked the night air, like a lurid lover – it became apparent to all that this was no domed building. It looked to be a giant, cigar-shaped balloon, tethered to a train engine.

The engine, itself, was of an extraordinary design. It was made of bronze, instead of iron. Intricate, swirling trimmings of gold ran its length, and a massive, gold propeller extended from its rear.

"Lawd, have mercy!" Ben whispered.

Margaret squeezed Harriet's hand tighter, as they followed the coachman onto the engine.

He flipped a switch on the wall and the engine was bathed in cool, amber light.

The driver removed his hat, bowed slightly, and spread his arms to the side. "Welcome to my airship! I call her *'The Nefertiti'!"*

Harriet ran her hands across the walls. They were constructed of wood, painted to look like sandstone. Strange, but beautiful runes of brass decorated the walls, ceiling and floor. "Beautiful work, Baas," she said.

"Thank you, Harriet," Baas replied.

He then turned his attention to Ben and Margaret. "Forgive me for not introducing myself sooner. We had to maintain a bit of anonymity until our arrival here. My name is Baas Bello: architect and captain of *The Nefertiti."*

Ben plopped down in a chair. The padded, soft leather was warm and comforting. "You called her an airship earlier. You mean to tell me, this thing *flies?"*

Baas laughed. "Yes, son! Oh, *how* she flies! Others have made airships – I am sure you have heard of the heated, air balloon. But none with the speed, carrying capacity and control of *The Nefertiti."*

"How *does* she fly, sir?" Margaret asked.

"She flies by steam," Baas replied. "Steam fills several balloons that are inside the 'cigar' floating above us. Assist the science with a bit of African animism and *voila!* She soars with the birds!"

A tall, athletically built, young man entered the engine. Ben studied him. The man's long, wavy hair and reddish-brown skin indicated strong Native American heritage, as well as black.

"The bags are loaded," the young man said.

"Excellent," Baas said. "Everyone, meet my son-in-law and apprentice: Talltrees."

Talltrees tipped his hat, and then walked to the back of the engine.

"Everyone, please, be seated," Baas said. Harriet and Margaret sat down next to Ben.

"We are about to depart," Baas began. "We will stop twice: for maintenance, to relieve ourselves and to rest. The trip should take us no more than two days, at best."

Baas moved to the front of the engine and took a seat in front of a bronze panel, with brass knobs and levers. A large, bronze wheel sat in the center of the panel. Baas gripped it and shouted: "Steam!"

Talltrees pulled a lever at the rear of the train engine. A hissing came from within the walls. After a moment, the engine jerked. Ben dug his fingers into the arms of his chair. Margaret let out a little yelp.

"Everything's fine," Baas shouted over the hissing noises. "We are just rising. When we reach our maximum altitude of a thousand feet, I will engage the exterior lights and the propeller.

"The what?" Ben asked.

"The flower-shaped contraption at the rear of the engine's exterior," Baas replied.

"Oh, thank you," Ben said.

Baas looked back at Ben and nodded. “As I was saying – I will engage the propeller and we will be on our way. If you get hungry or desire a drink, there is plenty jerked beef and water packed under your seats.”

Ben and Margaret stared out of the porthole in amazement, as the airship ascended high into the sky.

“We are flying, Aunt Harriet!” Margaret shouted. “We're *flying!”*

Harriet peeked out of her porthole. The massive field of wheat looked like a brown puzzle piece from that height. “Yes, child, we flyin’,” Harriet said. “We flyin,’ just like the angels, theyself.”

CHAPTER 18

April 28, 1865

Stanton stormed into the office of President Andrew Johnson. His hunters entered behind him.

Startled, President Johnson spilled his bourbon-laced coffee onto his lap. "Damn it!" President Johnson screamed. "What in the hell do you want, Secretary Stanton?" The President looked around the room at the hunters, who seemed a bit too comfortable in his office. "Who *are* these people?"

"Relax, Andy," Stanton replied, waving his hand as if to brush away the President's concerns.

He approached the desk. "I need *Warrior-One.*"

President Johnson slammed his fist down. "You barge into my office and discuss classified technology in front of…who the hell *are* they, Stanton?"

"My daughter has been abducted," said Stanton. "These people are going to help me get her back. I have intelligence that Margaret's abductors have gone to the deep South. I need *Warrior-One* to get there."

President Johnson wiped his trousers with a handkerchief. The stain spread wider. "Damn it!" He tossed the soiled handkerchief onto his desk. "I heard about your daughter. You have my condolences."

"Thank you."

President Johnson sat back in his chair. He stared at Stanton for a long while before he spoke again. "If I grant use of *Warrior-One,* I want something from you."

"Name your price."

"I want your resignation upon your return to Washington. I want Grant as Secretary of War."

Stanton stared into President Johnson's eyes. He did not blink. He did not move.

President Johnson lowered his gaze.

Stanton forced a smile. "Agreed."

President Johnson rose from his chair, and walked to a portrait of Abraham Lincoln. He removed the painting from the wall, revealing a safe. The door of the safe was small – about the dimensions of a small child's shoebox top – and had a combination lock comprised of five buttons: colored red, white, black, green and yellow.

The President pressed the buttons in a sequence, and the small door swung open. He reached into the safe and withdrew a cast iron key, nearly half the length of a man's forearm.

Stanton held out his hand and President Johnson slapped the key into his palm. The Secretary of War closed his fist around the key, and then turned to his hunters. "Alright, let's move!"

He headed toward the exit.

"Stanton..." President Johnson called after him.

Stanton snatched the office door open. "What?"

"This is a one way trip. Find your own way home!"

Stanton clinched his teeth. His hand squeezed the door handle until the circulation in his hands ceased. His knuckles went from dark tan to stark white. He slowly turned his face toward the President and stared him down.

President Johnson felt as if he had just swallowed a fistful of marbles. A rivulet of sweat, pooled at the crest of his head, made his scalp itch.

Stanton inhaled deeply, released the door handle and stormed out of the office.

President Johnson swallowed hard and exhaled. He felt a trickle of wetness roll down the back of his knee. He looked down.

The stain in his pants had grown even larger still, and bourbon-coffee was not the culprit.

CHAPTER 19

April 28, 1865

"Alright, everyone, listen up!" Baas shouted over the roar of the wind and the hiss of steam. "We are about to land and rest for a while!"

"Where are we?" Ben asked.

Harriet looked through a porthole. The green, flat land was familiar to her – as was most terrain in the states that lay east of the Mississippi River and a few west of it. "Kentucky," she said. "'round Perryville."

Talltrees stepped to the rear of the airship and pumped the throttle up and down in a choppy rhythm: *push-pull…push-pull…push-pull…push-pull…*

Steam hissed from the exhaust pipes with each sequence: *push-pull, hiss – push-pull, hiss…* and the airship descended smoothly.

Ben and Margaret stared out of the portholes, excited by the new technology and capabilities of *The Nefertiti.*

A cloud of steam rose from the engine's stack, and *The Nefertiti* landed in a flat field of grass. The field was surrounded by rolling hills and a meandering stream.

Baas swiveled in his chair to face his passengers. "We will depart in six hours. Stretch, relieve yourselves and relax. I am going to get some sleep.

Baas pulled a lever and the hum of the propeller ceased. "Please, do not make any noise louder than the din of conversation. We don' t want to attract any unnecessary attention."

Harriet nodded and stepped toward the engine door. Talltrees slid the door open. She looked around, peering into the distance. "We're clear. Let's go!"

Harriet helped Margaret down from the engine. Ben jumped out and Harriet followed.

Talltrees squatted in the engine's doorway. He slid his long, thick fingers across the black cherry wood. It was cool. Smooth. His fingers found a notch, which was just big enough to accommodate the tip of his middle finger. Inside the notch was a button. Talltrees pressed it and a panel slid back, revealing a compartment in the floor.

He reached into the compartment and withdrew a revolver. "Should I stand guard outside?"

"No need," Baas replied. "Harriet Tubman is out there."

CHAPTER 20

April 28, 1865

Warrior-One sped through the darkness, like a bullet through a barrel.

"Who could ever imagine!" Mama Maybelle exclaimed. "A train, runnin' in the bowels of the Earth?"

"Baas Bello could," Stanton replied.

Maybelle snickered. "That crazy, little African built this? He always was a smart one."

"He was commissioned by the British to build one in England," said Stanton. "He sold President Lincoln on the idea of a train that would run underground, in a system of tunnels that spanned from the White House; south, to Mexico and north, to Canada. The train was to be used only in the most dire threat to the President's life."

"Didn't do old Honest Abe much good, did it?" Caleb said, chuckling.

"Nope," Donald responded.

"A system of tunnels that expansive would take decades to build," Mr. Enthwhistle said.

"That was President Lincoln's concern," Stanton went on. "But he was shocked, when old Baas told him he had been *building* the tunnels for the past quarter century and was nearly done."

"Tracks and all?" Mr. Enthwhistle asked.

"Tracks and all," Stanton answered. "Why he did it – and *how* – no one knows. And Baas won't say."

Warrior-One spat a blast of steam from its stack, up through vents in the tunnel. To the denizens above-ground, the steam was a low fog, rolling along the surface.

"Who is this…this…*Box* fella' y'all talkin' 'bout?" Caleb asked.

"It's *Baas*," Stanton replied. "Baas Bello. He's believed to be the first person since the Christ to manifest gifts such as ours."

"The *second* person," Mama Maybelle interjected.

"My apologies, Mama Maybelle. Anyhow, his is the gift of invention, above and beyond anyone else on the planet. He's an engineer, a scientist, a witchdoctor... and as unpredictable as a drizzle in Spring."

CHAPTER 21

April 28, 1865

Harriet leaned against the airship, chewing a piece of beef jerky. Baas and Talltrees watched her through a porthole.

"She enjoys your jerked beef," Talltrees said, with a snicker.

"Do not be lewd," Baas replied. "She enjoys it because it is *like* her – tough, dark and salty."

"Sounds as if you are smitten."

Baas raised his small hand. "I'll smite *you*, if you do not hold your tongue!"

Talltrees sank down in his chair, covered his head with his arms and cowered, like a beaten whelp. A moment later, he peeked through his arms and smiled. Both men laughed.

"In all solemnity," Baas began."It has been a dark road I have traversed, since the passing of my beloved Hibernia. But I fear that no woman, not even Harriet, can replace her. I believe that…"

Talltrees squeezed Baas' shoulder, interrupting him. "Baas…look!"

Baas followed Talltrees' forefinger, which was pointed at something through the thick, wide, forward port.

In the distance were several swells of grass and vines, creeping toward *The Nefertiti.*

"Knolls!" Baas shouted.

The old man ran to the door of the engine and snatched it open. "Harriet," he screamed. *"Knolls* – at your three o'clock!"

Harriet snapped her head to the right. Upon spotting the ambulatory mounds of flora, she sprinted toward Ben and Margaret; who were busy forming their names out of small stones.

Ben saw Harriet's speedy approach and hopped to his feet. "Auntie Harriet, what's wrong?"

She snatched Margaret up and tossed the girl onto her shoulder. “Hey!” The child complained. “What is going on?”

“We got to go *now!* We trespassin’ on sorcerer’s land!”

Harriet turned on her heels and ran back toward the airship, with Ben following closely behind.

A jerky movement in Baas’ peripheral vision caught his attention. He stared out of the forward port. The knolls were standing up.

The creatures stood thrice the height of an average man. Chunks of dirt fell from their massive, grassy bodies as they shambled toward Harriet and the children.

The knolls were fearsome creatures. Their flesh and dense muscles were formed of soil and grass, which rested on a skeleton of stone – their eyes, swirling balls of red clay. Veins of vine ran, in an intricate network, throughout their frames; and they carried carved logs of hickory as their weapons.

In the center of each knolls' chest was a bronze clock the size of a dinner plate. The squadron roared in unison.

They had come for war.

Talltrees scurried to the notch in the floor of the engine. The panel slid open and he withdrew two Bello Revolving Rifles – weapons that looked like revolvers, but possessed a stock and a barrel the length of a carbine.

“Get up top and strap in!” Baas ordered. “I'm going to get *The Nefertiti* airborne once the children are on board!”

Talltrees quickly loaded six .58 caliber rounds into the cylinder of each rifle. He slung one rifle over his back, and leaped from the airship. After a brief moment, he peeked into the airship. “I love you, old man.”

“I love you too, son. Now *go!”*

Talltrees disappeared from view.

****

A knoll swung its gnarled club in a downward arc toward Harriet's head. She pulled Margaret tightly to her shoulder, and then somersaulted sideways to evade the blow.

The knoll's club pounded a crater into the ground, where Harriet had stood just moments before.

She plucked Margaret from her shoulder, and thrust her into Ben's arms. "Get to the airship!"

Margaret climbed onto Ben's back. He took off like a rocket – leaping and zigzagging to avoid the powerful slashes and thrusts of the knolls' hickory.

Harriet whipped her leg in a wide arc, striking a knoll in the lower leg with a sweeping, spinning roundhouse kick.

The creature's leg shattered. As did Harriet's.

Bits of gravel spewed from the knoll's stump as its foot separated from its leg. Blood ran, in rivulets, from Harriet's fractured leg. The knoll collapsed to its knees.

Harriet did not.

Instead, she hurled herself into the knoll's thick torso, slamming her shoulder into the clock embedded in its chest. The clock's face cracked. The creature howled – a sound like steam escaping from a tea kettle.

The sickening scent of chlorophyll and metal escaped its mouth.

She drove her fists into the cracked clock face. The thick glass shattered and the knoll fell onto its back, coughing up iron gears, copper wires and red dirt. The knoll shuddered once, twice... and was still.

Harriet limped toward *The Nefertiti.*

****

Another knoll lurched toward *The Nefertiti's* starboard side. Talltrees hurriedly strapped himself into a swivel chair that was bolted to the forward top of the airship. He whirled to his right and fired the Bello rifle.

A powerful, iron round coursed through the barrel and exploded from the muzzle. The round shattered the clock in the knoll's chest and it fell: never to rise again.

Talltrees quickly turned to his left and destroyed a second knoll, before it could bash *The Nefertiti's* port side with its club.

Ben made it to *The Nefertiti's* open door. He tossed Margaret inside the airship and then dived in behind her.

"Get in your seat, Margaret!" Baas ordered. "Ben, go to the aft wall and pull the toggle there! *Hurry* boy!"

Ben scrambled to the aft wall and slammed the lever down. The walls hissed. *The Nefertiti* jerked and began to rise.

"What about Auntie Harriet?" He asked.

"Here she comes, now," Baas replied. "She's going to have to jump though."

Ben looked out of a porthole. Harriet was limping briskly, but grimacing with each step. He noticed that her left leg was bent at an odd angle. The remaining four knolls were shambling after her.

"She's limpin,' Mr. Bello!" Ben screamed. "I think her leg's broke! She can't jump!"

Baas shook his head. "You don't know your Aunt Harriet, boy!"

Ben peeked through the porthole once more. Amazingly, Harriet was gaining distance between herself and the knolls. Her limp had already improved greatly.

A knoll's clock shattered and it fell, followed by another and another...

"Damned good shootin', Talltrees," Ben whispered.

Harriet leaped.

Her petite body, flying through the air, reminded Ben of a flying squirrel: leaping from branch to branch.

Harriet extended her arms and caught the floor of the doorway.

Ben rolled toward the doorway. "Auntie Harriet!"

Harriet's fingers began to slip on the smooth wood.

He reached out and grabbed Harriet's wrists and then struggled with all his might to pull her into the airship.

Harriet pushed against the side of the airship with her powerful right leg, driving her torso into the airship. Ben leaned back, straining his muscles as he pulled, and she slid into the airship. They fell on the floor of *The Nefertiti,* gasping for breath.

Talltrees, who had been watching Harriet struggle to enter the airship, held up his rifle in triumph. They had destroyed all of the knolls and everyone was safe.

Or so he thought.

One knoll remained. It had been shot, but its clock was still intact.

The monster rose up at the aft of the airship and swung its club in a wide arc. The club slammed into Talltrees' torso. The swivel chair – with Talltrees' limp body still strapped into it – ripped from the airship and plummeted to the ground below.

"No!" Baas screamed, as he watched a cloud of dirt rise from where his son-in-law had fallen.

The old genius engaged the propeller. The rotary came to life. Its blades tore into the knoll's chest. The knoll staggered backward, clutching at the hole where its clock once sat. It screamed weakly and fell.

Tears poured from Baas' eyes. He stared down at Talltrees' lifeless body, lying among the gravel, gears and dirt.

Baas brought his fingers to his brow in a salute. His son-in-law…his apprentice…his *friend* had fallen. "Full steam ahead, son. Full steam ahead."

CHAPTER 22

April 29, 1865

Warrior-One came to a stop. Stanton awoke from a peaceful sleep in the President's bed. He stretched and yawned.

"Slept like a babe, eh?" a voice said in the darkness.

Stanton pressed a switch in the bed's headboard, and the Presidential Cabin lit up. Mr. Enthwhistle was standing at the foot of the bed.

"Mr. Enthwhistle," Stanton said, as he sat up. "What is it?"

"The engineer announced that we are in Galveston."

The Secretary of War rose from the bed, and strapped on his gun belt. "Alright... this station is below a barn on the outskirts of town. There should be horses there, and we will procure a cart for Maybelle. We'll go to town, get rooms and lay low, until we start the hunt this evening."

Mr. Enthwhistle nodded and was gone.

Stanton threw on his topcoat and headed out of the cabin. He walked through the car, admiring its opulence and its ingenious design. It contained a study library, dining room and a parlor. All were crafted from the finest silks, leathers, velvets, mahogany, ivory and gold. And he had ridden in it before that fool, Andrew Johnson. As was fitting.

One day, the ungifted would bow to the will of their gifted masters. One day soon. *Me, resign? Bah!*

President Johnson needed to learn one truth that had stood since the dawning of the first civilization. Rule was determined by military might – and none was mightier than Edwin M. Stanton, Secretary of War.

Stanton entered the guest car, where his hunters awaited him. "Good morning," he greeted them. "As you all know, we have arrived in Galveston, Texas. Let us all try to remain as incognito as possible up there."

Caleb removed his hat, scratched his head and pointed in the direction of Mama Maybelle, who was enjoying a gallon of fresh-squeezed orange juice. "Now, how in high-Hell is a seven foot tall niggra gal…er…*woman* in Galveston, Texas, of all places, gonna stay – what you call it – incog*negro*?"

"That's incog*nito*, Caleb," Stanton replied, shaking his head. "Obviously, we'll have to work a bit harder to protect Mama Maybelle's anonymity.

Mama Maybelle waved her hands, which were as large as a man's head, and smiled. "Aw, child, Mama will be just fine. I been hidin' in plain sight since befo' America was *called* America."

"So, it was just you and the Injuns, huh?" Caleb asked with a sneer.

"Boy, it was me and my folks that greeted the first Red Man, come down here from Asia."

Caleb shook his head and scowled. "Next, you'll be tellin' us *you* made the Grand Canyon!"

"Naw, child," Mama Maybelle retorted. "*That* was my grandpa."

Everyone burst into laughter. Caleb threw up his hands in resignation.

"Alright, people," Stanton said. "Let's go. Galveston awaits."

Mama Maybelle slid open the door of the train car and the hunters exited.

Stanton placed a hand on her arm. "Mama, a word?"

Maybelle nodded and stepped back into the car. "Yes, child?"

"Mama, I know you have endured much on this trip. The incident in Washington, D.C.; Caleb's racist remarks. My apologies; but I promise you, it will be well worth it in the end."

“Don’t fret, child,” Mama Maybelle said. The gargantuan woman walked to the door of the car. “Let’s just bring my grandbaby, home!”

“Yes, mama.”

CHAPTER 23

April 29, 1865

Sand slapped Harriet's face, as she leaped from *The Nefertiti* into the arid heat of San Antonio.

She thrust her hand inside her overcoat, and pulled out a pair of worn goggles. "Ben…Margaret…" Harriet shouted over the howling winds. "Goggles on!"

Ben and Margaret donned their goggles, and departed the airship.

Baas stepped down from *The Nefertiti.* His face was a mask of loss; of regret. "Ben, head starboard side. You'll find a panel there. Open it. Your bags are inside."

"Yes, sir," Ben replied. The young man sprinted to the front of the airship, and disappeared as he ran toward the right.

Harriet studied Baas for a moment. "Baas, I'm an old warhorse, an' old warhorses ain't much for words. But know that Talltrees did you an' yo' daughter *proud*."

"What am I going to tell my baby, Harriet?"

"Tell her that her husband died a good death. A *soldier's* death. And the Lawd got a special place in heaven fo' his soldiers."

"I should have trained him better," Baas replied.

"You trained that boy just fine," Harriet said. "Never seen a better shot. We *soldiers*, Baas. We *die*. It's up to us to make sure he didn't die in vain."

Baas clinched his fists, and stared at the sand dancing about his feet. "You mean…the sorcerer."

"I ain't never seen knolls that big or that strong," Harriet replied. "We dealin' with a powerful sorcerer in Perryville. An alchemist of the highest order."

She patted Baas on the shoulder. "After I'm done with this business in Mexico, I'll help you find him and send him on his way."

Baas hugged Harriet. His tears spotted the shoulder of her overcoat. "Thank you," he replied.

Baas released his embrace as Ben returned with the bags. "Walk east about a half mile," he began. "There's an old shack there. You will find food and water inside. Sinai will meet you there in a few hours to take you into Mexico."

Baas climbed back into *The Nefertiti.* "I will fly back over this area every five days for a month. After that…"

"Understood," Harriet replied with a nod.

Baas waved goodbye and closed T*he Nefertiti's* door. It locked with a soft click.

Harriet took Margaret's hand and grabbed her bag. She peered through the dense cloud of sand to the sky above it.

"I know Death is on our tail, Lawd," Harriet said. "Thank you for taking us *this* far. But I ask that you walk with us a little while longer, Lawd. Just a little while longer."

CHAPTER 24

April 29, 1865

"Try again!" Stanton slammed a gloved fist into a hitching post. The post shook in protest.

Druga sniffed the air again. She shook her head, as she lightly bit her bottom lip. "There is no trace of your daughter here. We have checked every side of town. I assure you, comrade, she is *not* in Galveston."

"You *assured* me Harriet Tubman's father spoke the truth!" Stanton shouted. "You were *wrong*!"

He rocked on his heels as he listened to his gut. It never failed him. Finally, it seemed, Stanton's gut spoke – and spoke loudly. His eyes widened, and his scowl showed traces of a smile fighting its way to the surface. "You were *not* wrong, Druga. Miss Tubman *lied!* She told her parents Galveston, knowing they'd be questioned."

Stanton punched his palm with his fist, and the scowl beat back the smile. "Damn it!" he screamed. "Margaret could be anywhere!"

"We'll find her, child," Mama Maybelle assured him. "With your resources, word of your Margaret will get back to you *real* soon."

The Secretary of War took a deep breath. "Okay, let's rest up for now." He pointed at a building across the street from them. The sign on the structure read, simply: *SALOON.* "That saloon across the way has rooms."

Caleb and Donald mounted their horses. "Me and Donald will be back shortly," Caleb said. "There's a cathouse down a ways. We're gonna get us a little cooch. Care to join us, Druga?"

Druga growled. Her powerful jaw clenched, as she bared her fangs.

"Alright," Caleb chuckled, raising his hands in mock surrender. "Suit yourself." The twins rode off laughing.

"Disgusting!" Druga hissed.

"Let's go," Stanton said.

The hunters followed him to the saloon. The Secretary of War stopped a few feet from the entrance. "Mama Maybelle," he called.

"Yes, child?"

"Take my bags," Stanton said, pointing to his trunk. "The story is: you are my former slave; now working as my maid."

"Good idea, child." Maybelle picked up everyone's baggage and tucked them under her massive arms.

They entered the saloon. The music from the worn piano and the chatter, decrescendoed as the patrons of the saloon took notice of the motley clan.

"Welcome to the *Lucky Seven Saloon and Inn!*" the bartender shouted with a smile.

"Hold on, Johnny-Ray," a customer ordered. The man stood up. He was tall and lean. His Confederate uniform was freshly washed, and every wrinkle had been beaten out of it. "Ain't no niggers allowed in here!"

"She works for me," Stanton replied, affecting his best Southern accent.

"She sure is a mountain of mud, ain't she?" Someone shouted.

The men in the saloon burst into laughter. The odor of alcohol, sweat and filth overwhelmed Druga. She covered her nose and mouth to ward off the sickening smells.

A man with dirty fingers – sitting at a table of gamblers near her – patted Druga's butt. "For good luck," the man sneered. The other gamblers snickered.

Mr. Enthwhistle slammed his cane onto the gamblers' table. Cards and coins scattered all over the table and the floor. "Do *not* touch the ladies, mate!"

The patrons in the bar leaped to their feet.

Mama Maybelle put the hunters' luggage down and slowly tilted her head from side to side, touching an ear to each shoulder. "That ol' train ride got Mama all stiff. I reckon this would be a good time to stretch out a bit."

Stanton gently pressed down on Mr. Enthwhistle's upraised cane. The Englishman lowered the cane and pressed it against his thigh.

"I am going outside to have a smoke," Stanton said. "Care to join me?"

Mr. Enthwhistle nodded and then followed Stanton out of the saloon, leaving Mama Maybelle and Druga inside to get better acquainted with the locals.

CHAPTER 25

April 29, 1865

Ben watched Harriet and Margaret as they slept. Margaret was restless, tossing to and fro; legs kicking; arms flailing.

The knolls had frightened her beyond imagination. "Reanimated souls of fallen soldiers" is how Baas had described them. The monstrous offspring of magic and science.

Ben prayed to never again share the same space with one of their ilk. He crawled to a window and peeked outside. "Not much to see," he whispered. "Sand…a big cactus…stones…and…a…horse?"

The teenager squinted his eyes, and craned his neck to get a clearer look. It was, indeed, a horse... and its riders were nearby. A man and a woman lay on a blanket making love. Their ruddy skins melding into one, as they gyrated and undulated in unison.

Ben pried the door open, and slipped quietly out of the dilapidated old shack. He lay on his belly and then slithered towards the couple. His hand inched toward the knife that was tucked into the waistband of his trousers.

The couple – lost in the throes of ecstasy – did not notice Ben closing on them.

He gritted his teeth and exploded forward. There was a quick flash of metal and then…blood... spurt after spurt.

The man clutched at the jagged incision in his neck. Blood sprayed between his fingers, and into his woman's face. The woman's eyes popped open. She tried to scream as her man collapsed onto her chest. But Ben's hand was upon her mouth, smothering her cries.

A shiver ran up his spine and as he sank his knife into the woman's soft, quivering belly, he was delighted to feel his penis go fully erect against his inner thigh.

“A masterpiece,” Ben hissed. “One that demands the artist’s signature.”

And the engraving upon flesh began.

CHAPTER 26

April 29, 1865

The twins dismounted their horses, and approached Stanton and Mr. Enthwhistle, who were relaxing outside. Their faces were painted with identical grins.

"Y'all just missed out on the best cooch in the South," Caleb said. "Ain't that right, brother?"

"Yup," Donald replied.

Stanton blew a ring of smoke into the air, and Mr. Enthwhistle puffed on his pipe. The smell of sweet tobacco filled the air.

Caleb looked around. A confused expression was on his face. "Why are you two just standin' around out here? And where are the ladies?"

The door of the saloon flew open. A man toppled out of the saloon, and landed in a broken and twisted mass at Caleb's feet.

"They're inside," Stanton calmly replied.

Caleb and Donald ran into the saloon, weapons at the ready.

"Damn," Caleb whispered.

The saloon was a mess of limbs, entrails, blood and bile.

Maybelle stood at the bar. A bottle of whiskey was pressed to her lips.

On the stool beside her sat a man's head. A penis lolled in his mouth in place of a tongue.

Druga reclined against the wall at Maybelle's rear. She sniffed the air as she picked human flesh from her teeth. "Mama Maybelle, there is one more...Behind the bar."

Suddenly, a pudgy, little man rose from behind the bar. A double-barreled shotgun was cradled in his arms.

Caleb raised his revolvers and Donald aimed his rifle. But before they could get off a shot, the man's head left his body. The man's head – propelled by Mama Maybelle's powerful backhand slap – flew past the bar, and lodged in the wall at the back of the saloon.

The man's headless body disappeared behind the bar, and hit the floor with a wet thud.

Mama Maybelle looked down at her dress, which was covered in blood. "Goodness, look at me! Mama got to get cleaned up!"

The giantess turned from the bar and headed toward the stairs. "Caleb, be a good boy and bring Mama's bag upstairs."

Caleb looked around the bar and shook his head. He had sent many men on their way, but never with such brutality – such ferocity. He admired the women's work.

The cowboy searched the bar, until he found a cotton bag with yellow flowers embroidered upon it. "Yes, ma'am. Right away."

CHAPTER 27

April 29, 1865

Harriet tapped Ben's calf with the back of her hand. "Wake up, Ben! There's a wagon approachin!'"

Ben feigned awakening. He fought the urge to laugh, as he stretched his limbs and yawned convincingly. "We leavin' now, Auntie Harriet?"

"I think so," she replied. "Gather up our things."

Harriet peeked out of the window, as he stuffed their belongings into their respective bags. An old cart slowly approached the shack. The horse was – in contrast to the cart – young and muscular: with a shiny, well-groomed coat the color of roasted chestnut.

The driver, however, appeared to be as old and worn as the cart he drove.

"Sinai..." Harriet called.

Sinai waved his large, calloused hand. She picked up Margaret, cradled the girl in her arms and ran to the cart.

Ben skipped happily behind them.

"Moses!" Sinai exclaimed as he stepped down from the cart. "It's been a long time..."

Harriet gave him a warm hug. She held on to him for a long while and inhaled deeply. He smelled of jasmine, agave and watermelon, as always. "It's been *too* long! I see you're still wearing that cologne."

"Yep. I figure if it could mask the stench of that old Nosferatu, it could make an old scout-guide like me smell wonderful!"

"I hear you done settled now," Harriet said. "Callin' Mexico home.

Sinai nodded. His thick, kinky locks tap-danced upon his shoulders and soft-shoed across his face. “Gone native, yes; but a scout and guide can’t ever really be settled. It’s contrary to the job.

She nodded. “I suppose it is.”

Harriet grabbed Ben and Margaret by their wrists, and pulled them before the old wagon master. “This is my nephew Ben. And this here is my niece, Margaret.”

“Nephew Ben and…umm…*niece* Margaret,” Sinai said with a wink. “Pleasure to meet you.”

“Likewise,” Ben replied.

“Pleased to meet you, sir,” Margaret said.

“Now, y’all gon’ get in,” Harriet said, pointing at the wagon. “We ‘bout to leave.” They climbed into the covered wagon.

Sinai climbed back into the drivers’ seat and then offered his hand to Harriet. “Ride shotgun, so we can talk a spell.”

She took Sinai’s hand. The old man pulled and Harriet jumped: spinning her body into a somersault over Sinai’s head, and landing in the seat beside him.

“Show off,” he said, shaking his head. Harriet smiled. Sinai snapped the reins and his horse began to trot. He snapped the reins again and the horse began to run.

Ben looked back at the old shack and at the ground where the young lovers had lain together…had bled…had suffered.

His erection returned and he smiled. *Mexico, here we come!*

CHAPTER 28

April 29, 1865

The noon heat crashed, in waves, through Galveston. Stanton looked down from the window of his room.

The Union Army's Intelligence Division, led by Lieutenant Colonel Conger, were busy tossing large crates into several wagons. The soldiers – dressed as civilians for discretion – had sanitized the saloon quite nicely.

Broken furniture had been replaced. Blood and flesh had been scrubbed away.

The *Lucky Seven Saloon's* "real" owner, Clarence Taylor, was behind the bar, ready to greet patrons with a smile. All of this was enforced by Victor Leach; who did his own special brand of cleaning – wiping clean the recent memories of the good citizens of Galveston, and implanting new ones.

No one in Galveston – save Stanton and his hunters – had any recollection of the grisly massacre at the saloon; which had taken place mere hours ago.

Leach did amazing work, but at a hefty price. He was a cannibal, who had a particular liking for the flesh of little, Asian boys. Stanton hated him, and kept the cannibal under constant surveillance. He'd vowed to kill Leach one day... after a long session of torture, of course.

Colonel Conger rode up to the saloon on his horse. He dismounted quickly and exchanged words with one of the men on the street, who pointed up toward Stanton's window.

He spotted Stanton in the window and snapped to attention: delivering a crisp salute, which Stanton returned.

"Morning, Colonel Conger!" the Secretary of War shouted.

“Morning, sir!” Colonel Conger yelled back. “Secretary Stanton, I have word of your daughter’s whereabouts!”

Stanton’s heart jumped. He leaned further out the window. “Then hurry on up here, man!”

He ran to his door, unlocked it and snatched it open. Colonel Conger sprinted up the stairs and into his room.

After exchanging another quick salute, Stanton gestured toward the circular desk in the corner of his room. “Grab a seat.”

Colonel Conger removed a chair from the desk and placed it a couple of feet from Stanton, who sat on his bed.

“What news do you have, Colonel?”

“A few hours ago, in San Antonio, a horse rode into town. A girl was tied to it with strips from her dress, and from a man’s trousers – the man that the horse was dragging behind it.”

Stanton’s eyes narrowed to slits and his jaw tightened. “Go on.”

“The man had bled to death from a laceration of the carotid artery. The girl, however, lived for an hour after arriving in San Antonio. She eventually died of shock from her wounds, which were quite extensive and…odd.”

“Odd?”

“The letters ‘J.B.’ were carved into her torso. Puncture wounds between each letter, indicate they were initials.”

“Initials?” Stanton echoed. “John Booth?”

“Not likely. The girl described the perpetrator as a Negro male, in his early twenties at most. She also said the Negro kept chanting one word, over and over, as he cut her.”

“What word? Spit it out, man!” Stanton ordered.

“Margaret.”

Stanton leaped to his feet. “Good work, Colonel! Upon my return to Washington – *after* I deal with Andy Johnson – I will see to your promotion to full Colonel.”

“Thank you, sir!” Colonel Conger said, as he snapped to attention and saluted.

Stanton returned the salute. “Tell the hunters to meet me in the saloon. We leave immediately for San Antonio!”

CHAPTER 29

April 30, 1865

Laughter, a gentle breeze and the succulent smell of mesquite grilled chicken filled the air of Punta Blanca. The tiny Mexican village was home to some of the friendliest, and most supportive people Harriet had ever met.

Theirs was a bond built in blood.

Punta Blanca was once the favored hunting ground of the dreaded Were-Coyotes.

The villagers of Punta Blanca had defended themselves against the Were-Coyotes for decades; and had become so proficient at killing shape-shifters, that a lycanthrope hunter with training in Punta Blanca demanded a hefty purse for his or her services.

Sinai had come to Punta Blanca for such training and never left.

Father Ramon – the village priest and its unofficial leader – handed Harriet a glass filled with an amber liquid. “Try this, Harriet. It is my signature creation: Agave wine.”

Harriet placed her lips to the glass and took a sip. The wine was sweet...exquisite. She took another sip. “Padre, the Lawd has certainly guided yo’ hand aright!”

Father Ramon laughed. “Well, there's plenty. Perhaps the wine and our great food will convince you to stay.”

“The Lawd say a week is all I got,” Harriet said, pointing at Margaret, who was busy attacking a cob of roasted corn. “The child will be back in the hands of her daddy by then. And I’ll be on my way to make due on a promise I made to an old friend.”

“Well, should you ever change your…”

Father Ramon’s words grew heavy in Harriet’s ears.

Punta Blanca began to slowly spin.

Harriet looked to the sky. The moon contracted to a silver dot and grew dim and then…

Darkness.

The sound of thunder penetrated the darkness and a flash of lightning illuminated it.

Harriet looked upon the horizon. Fast approaching were the skeletons of huge horses with the tails of scorpions. Upon each horse rode a hooded reaper, armed with a scythe.

She turned to run, but her feet were too heavy... she could only manage, with great effort, to drag her boots along the sandy ground.

The skeletal horses drew closer. Closer.

The earth began to shake…to collapse.

Harriet awakened. Ben was splashing water from a cup onto the back of her neck. The music and laughter had stopped. All eyes in the village were on Harriet.

She stood up. "Father Ramon…Sinai…get everyone to the church!" They exchanged confused glances.

"Now!" Harriet demanded. "Death is comin' and He comin' *fast*!"

"Then, we stand and fight!" Father Ramon replied.

The villagers shouted in agreement.

"What is comin' ain't no shape-shifter," Harriet said. It's worse. *Much* worse. Run to the church! Hide! If it get past me, then you just might get that fight you itchin' fo'!"

Father Ramon hopped onto a bench and addressed the villagers. "Gather your weapons and get to the church! We will let Harriet handle this as she sees fit! *Go!"*

The villagers moved like a well-oiled machine – some ushering the smaller children to the church – while others gathered the shotguns and revolvers. The older children snatched up fistfuls of silver bullets, and buckshot from crates as they ran to the church.

Harriet nudged Margaret toward Ben. “Get to the church, Ben!”

“Yes, ma’am...!” The young man grabbed Margaret’s hand and they sprinted off.

Sinai loaded his shotgun and then stuffed a box of sixteen-gauge buckshot into each pocket of his duster.

“Sinai, take cover,” Harriet whispered. “They close.”

Sinai ran toward a large wooden water barrel and crouched behind it.

Suddenly, a crimson mist rose from Harriet’s back and she collapsed onto her belly. Droplets of blood rained down on the plates of chicken and corn on the cob.

“Harriet!” Sinai hissed. “Are you okay?”

She began crawling on her belly, toward a fruit cart a few yards away. “I’ll be fine... I been shot. Shoulder’s broken. It’ll take a few minutes to heal.”

“Harriet, out here, you can hear a gunshot from a mile away!” Sinai said. “I didn’t hear a thing! How can someone hit from that far, and with *what* kind of weapon?”

Harriet’s face was like stone, masking her pain. Her eyes shrank to slivers. “Wasn’t no ordinary man made that shot. He been brushed.”

“Like you?”

“Naw, nothin’ like me,” said Harriet. “Some folks is brushed by the hand o’ God. Some folks brushed by that *Other* One. Whoever made that shot been brushed by the Other One.”

The sound of many hooves striking the earth echoed throughout the village.

“I see them Harriet!” Sinai said. “Five on horses and a coach!”

“Stay still and be quiet!” She ordered.

She shifted her focus to the clouds. "Lawd, I know you done made the blind see an' the deaf hear. So, I reckon it's within yo' power to do the contrary."

Harriet clenched her fists and bowed her head. "Shut their eyes, Lawd. Close their ears. Hoodwink and stun them, Master. An' if you see fit, bless me to kill them all! Amen, Lawd. Amen."

"Amen," Sinai echoed.

A dust cloud rolled across the tiny village as the horsemen charged in.

CHAPTER 30

April 30, 1865

Stanton scanned the village. There were several long tables of half-eaten food, and small houses made of adobe, with no movement inside them. A large church, with a huge, silver door and a silver bell in its tower, stood as the village's centerpiece…

Lying on the ground, with a large hole in the back of her skull, was Harriet Tubman.

Donald grinned proudly, and held up his Sharps Carbine.

"Good shootin,' brother!" Caleb shouted.

"Yup," Donald replied.

Druga sniffed the air and shook her head. "There is something wrong. I smell much fear, but no death. I believe…"

She was interrupted by the sight of Donald's throat bursting open.

Blood and bits of Donald's flesh painted Caleb's vest. Donald slumped forward and then fell from his horse. His lifeless fingers still clutched his carbine.

Caleb leaped from his horse and knelt beside his lifeless twin. He felt as if a part of him had been erased; like a hole was in his gut…but the hole felt, somehow…heavy.

"Donald, don't *leave* me like this! Don't leave me – *Donny!"*

"Who is shooting?" Mr. Enthwhistle asked.

Druga sniffed the air once more. "There is no smell of gunpowder! Something is *wrong* here!"

Stanton squinted and his brow furrowed as he examined his surroundings, calling forth the gift he called "Understanding." Suddenly, Understanding came to him and he *knew*. "It is Harriet! The old witch has conjured a glamour. She's *not* dead!"

"She *will* be shortly!" Caleb screamed, as he rose to his feet, firing both revolvers furiously in all directions. Within the span of a second, Caleb had fired a score of rounds, regenerating bullets in his revolvers through the force of his will.

The bullets tore through cacti, the bell in the tower and even the earth beneath Caleb's feet. Something hot whizzed by Caleb's ear, taking a sliver of flesh from his earlobe with it. Caleb rolled to his left, just avoiding another shot. "*Show* yourself, witch!" He shouted as he pressed his fingers to his mangled ear.

A round penetrated the side of Mama Maybelle's coach, and lodged in her seat – an inch from her belly. *Well, I'll* be. *Mama almost got hit. We can't have that!*

The giantess coiled her back, bending forward deeply, and then exploded upward. The roof exploded into dust, as her powerful legs propelled her through it and high into the sky.

She raised her right hand high above her head, and arched her back.

As she landed, Mama Maybelle slammed her thick palm into the ground. The earth shook and a wave of sand and soil exploded, in a wide path, from her palm to where the glamour of Harriet's lifeless body lay.

Everything in the path of the devastating shockwave was propelled into the air, or burst into pieces from the force of the seismic tremor.

Harriet's illusion faded as she was hurled into the church door. Her back slammed into the thick, silver door and the air swiftly evacuated her lungs through her nostrils.

Druga sniffed the air. She caught the scent of jasmine, agave and watermelon. "There! Someone is hiding there!" She shouted, pointing to the water barrel, behind which Sinai had taken cover.

Sinai intended to fire his weapon; but Mr. Enthwhistle had drawn the sword concealed within his cane and thrust it through the back of Sinai's neck, before the old scout-guide had a chance to move.

The end of the sword protruded from Sinai's wide open mouth. The tip of the sword lodged into the water barrel. A clear river of water ran from the water barrel, down the length of Mr. Enthwhistle's sword and into Sinai's mouth.

Harriet forced herself to one knee, and then fired her revolver at Enthwhistle's head. But the Englishman vanished before the iron round could touch him.

Mr. Enthwhistle reappeared right in front of Harriet, and slashed at her face with his sword.

She rolled backwards, evading the slash, and popped to her feet.

The Englishman slashed again.

Harriet deflected the blow with her left hand. She grabbed Mr. Enthwhistle's wrist in a powerful grip and aimed her gun at his head. He knocked the gun aside, and then took control of Harriet's wrist in a grip of his own.

She hammered a vicious barrage of knee strikes into Enthwhistle's thighs. The bones in his upper legs snapped, and he collapsed forward – his legs at odd and sickening angles. Mr. Enthwhistle screamed as he fell onto his side, writhing in pain.

Harriet fired three rounds into his chest.

Mr. Enthwhistle spasmed violently...once…twice. And then he lay still.

Caleb fired a volley of bullets. Harriet whirled, leaped, dived and rolled, evading every shot.

Several bullets lodged in the church door. One round shattered the transom's window above the door. Moments later a child's scream broke the silence within the church.

"Stand down, Caleb!" Stanton ordered. "That may be Margaret in there!"

Caleb raised his revolvers once more. "Stand down, my *ass!* That nigger bitch killed my brother!"

Stanton drew a cigar from inside his topcoat. "Fire that weapon again and you're dead."

Caleb whirled around to face Stanton. He pointed his guns at the Secretary of War's head. "I'll blow your ass right off that horse, you threaten me again, Stanton!"

Stanton calmly lit his cigar. He took a long draw from the huge stogie...and blew a cloud of smoke directly at Caleb's guns...and the hands holding them.

Caleb screamed in agony as needles of pain ripped through his fists.

The cowboy could only stare in horror, as the flesh of his hands melted away from the bones. Skin and muscle landed on Caleb's boots in a steaming pile. He fell to his knees, his body convulsing as shock overtook him.

With Caleb no longer a threat, Stanton returned his focus to Harriet. He drew his pistol and searched the area. She was nowhere in sight.

"Where is she?"

"Don't know, child," Mama Maybelle answered. "During your spat with Caleb, the little mouse scampered away. Gotta be close, though."

Druga sniffed the air. "Harriet is in the church. She must have sneaked in while we were… preoccupied."

"Mama Maybelle," Stanton said, smiling. "Open up the church, please."

The titan studied Caleb's horse for a moment, and then rubbed her hands together gleefully. "Comin' right up, child. Mama will have us in there in no time!"

CHAPTER 31

April 30, 1865

The mahogany benches of the church were arranged in a V-shape, with its closed end pointing toward the pulpit. The open end of the "V" faced the door. The villagers knelt behind the pews, aiming their weapons over the backs of the benches and at the door.

Father Ramon and Harriet stood in the pulpit. "Is there any other way out of the church?" She asked.

Father Ramon tilted his head toward the entrance. A lock of curly, white hair fell onto his forehead. "That door is the only way in or out. Makes it easier to defend against the
Were-Coyotes."

She scowled. "Also makes it easier to trap you in here."

"Well, what would you suggest we…"

Suddenly, the thick, silver door flew off its hinges and sped towards the pulpit.

Harriet pushed Father Ramon out of the door's path, and then somersaulted sideways over it. The door crashed into the rear wall.

Caleb's horse followed right behind the door – cannonballing across the church. The horse landed in the pulpit, it's tongue flailing from side to side. The animal's belly spasmed and then it went limp.

Mama Maybelle stood where the door once was.

Framed by the doorway, Maybelle looked – to Harriet – like a portrait of power. And death.

"Knock, knock," the giant said, smiling.

Harriet aimed her revolver at Mama Maybelle's broad chest. The giantess leaped upward, disappearing from view as Harriet fired. The bullet whizzed across the village square. A cloud of sawdust rose in the distance, when the bullet found a home in a hitching post.

Mama Maybelle suddenly crashed through the ceiling, landing inches from Harriet.

Harriet brought her revolver up to Maybelle's face.

She slapped the revolver from Harriet's hand – her weapon flew across the church; bounced off a wall and fell to the floor. Mama Maybelle raised her fist and brought it down forcefully, toward the top of Harriet's head.

Harriet swiftly side-stepped, avoiding the powerful strike.

Mama Maybelle's fist struck a pew. The mahogany bench shattered.

A hard blow struck Harriet in the chest and she stumbled backward.

Druga landed in a crouched position after delivering the flying side-kick to Harriet's torso. The Russian huntress darted forward, and threw a vicious spear-hand thrust at Harriet's right eye.

Harriet blocked the blow, parrying it to her inside.

Druga fell slightly off balance, pulled by Harriet's forceful parry.

Harriet delivered a punishing right hook to the Russian woman's exposed left side. The brutal strike resounded with a sickening crunch, as two of Druga's ribs shattered.

The huntress grimaced as she collapsed onto her left knee. She opened her mouth wide, baring her wicked teeth, and sank them deeply into Harriet's thigh. Harriet screamed, and pounded the back of her fist into Druga's jaw.

Druga slid down the aisle and rolled under a pew.

Harriet returned her attention to Mama Maybelle, who was busy tearing off the limbs and heads from terrified villagers. Harriet leaped toward the colossus and battered her in the nose with a crushing head-butt. Blood sprayed out in a web across Maybelle's face.

The giant quickly grabbed Harriet's head with both hands, trapping it in a vice-like grip.

Mama Maybelle squeezed.

Harriet felt her eyes bulge and the veins in her skull constrict. She struggled to remain conscious; but the increasing pressure on her head made it nearly impossible and darkness rushed to meet her.

"Child," Mama Maybelle began. "Mama ain't been bled since long befo' you was born."

A trickle of blood leaked from Harriet's left ear.

"I like it, though..." the giantess continued. "Let's an old woman know she still alive!"

Stanton entered the church. "Margaret! Margaret, it's daddy!"

She stood up from her hiding place behind a pew. *"Daddy!"*

Stanton smiled warmly and opened his arms. Margaret lurched forward in an attempt to run to him. But someone grabbed her arm, stopping her.

Ben stood and pulled her close to him.

"Ben," Margaret cried. "It's alright! That is my daddy and…!"

"Shut up!" Ben screamed. He pressed his knife to Margaret's throat.

He leered at Stanton. "Tell that demon to let Harriet go, or I'll slit this little bitch's throat!"

"J.B., I presume," Stanton said calmly. "Let my daughter go now and you have my word, I will let you live."

Ben pressed harder with the knife. Margaret whimpered as a line of blood ran down her neck. "Since you know who I am, you know what I'm capable of! Let Harriet go, *now*! I won't ask again!"

Mama Maybelle released Harriet.

Harriet collapsed onto her knees. She breathed deeply and relaxed, so her body could begin to heal from the extensive damage she had sustained.

Ben continued to hold Margaret close. He laughed heartily as he pointed at Stanton with his knife. "You played your part well…as did you all."

He pushed Margaret toward Stanton. The Secretary of War embraced his daughter, as tears flowed from his eyes.

Ben took a bow. "Now, *this* act has come to an end. And soon, the final curtain will too, close."

Stanton glared at Ben. "Booth!"

Harriet opened her eyes and stared at him. She could not believe what she was hearing. Ben did not sound like himself and – perhaps – he *wasn't* himself at all.

"*Everyone drop your weapons*," A voice from the doorway commanded.

Ben dropped his knife and raised his hands above his head. "And that – ladies and gentlemen," he said grinning, " – is my cue!"

He walked toward the doorway.

Standing before him was a Captain of the Mexican Army. Ben looked over the Captain's shoulder. Behind him stood a company of battle-hardened soldiers.

Ben giggled with glee. Everything was falling into place quite nicely.

The gods were finally smiling upon him.

CHAPTER 32

May 1, 1865

The cell was dank and reeked of mildew. Harriet coughed to clear her lungs of the malignance in the air.

She examined her surroundings. Secretary of War, Edwin Stanton was in a cell by himself. The giant, black woman and the white girl, with teeth like a dog shared a cell. Ben – or whoever it was that *looked* like Ben – was alone in the last cell.

"Booth," Stanton yelled. "I do not know how you have changed bodies or what you are up to, and I do not care! However, I assure you I shall repay you, in kind, for all that you have done!"

Ben leaped from his bunk, and pressed his face as far between the bars as he could force it. "You have no *idea* all that I have done!" His face twisted into a sardonic grin. "You are just a pawn on the chessboard, Stanton!"

"And what are you?" Stanton asked. "The queen?"

"Why, I'm the man moving the pieces, boy!"

Stanton spat on the cell floor. "Booth, I am…"

"Don't call me that!" Ben screamed.

Harriet studied his voice, his face. Everything about him was familiar, but…wrong. It was *not* Ben. But still, someone she knew well.

And then, it came to her.

As Ben grew more twisted, more *dark,* she knew.

"Naw, it can't be!" she gasped.

He threw back his head and laughed. "What is it, General Tubman? You look as if you've seen a ghost."

"You ain't Ben…*or* Booth!" Harriet exclaimed.

He grinned.

"Then who in the hell *is* he?" Stanton demanded.

"An old friend," Harriet whispered. "John Brown."

CHAPTER 33

May 1, 1865

Corporal Manuel Alejandro Rivera lay in the infirmary, counting the mosquitoes on the ceiling. For three years, he had served faithfully under Captain Vega on the battlefield; not once was he injured or fall ill.

And then, in peacetime, he fell from his horse and shattered both ankles."Such luck," Corporal Rivera whispered. "I guess things can't get any *worse*."

The door to Corporal Rivera's room opened with a squeak.

He was about to be proven wrong. Things *were* about to get worse. *Much* worse.

The Corporal turned his face toward the door. What now stood in his room at once sickened, frightened and enraged him. He opened his mouth to scream. But a cold, skeletal hand covered his mouth, trapping the screams in the young soldier's throat.

The intruder's other hand tore a piece of flesh from Corporal Rivera's bicep. The creature tossed the meat into its mouth and began chewing. Rivera's eyes rolled back in their sockets and he convulsed, as waves of pain washed over him.

The decaying creature tipped its coachman hat and smiled, as it swallowed the good Corporal's skin and sinew. "How *do*, amigo?" The intruder began. "My name's Caleb, Caleb Butler…and I got a job for you!"

CHAPTER 34

May 1, 1865

"John Brown is dead," Stanton said. "I attended his hanging and watched him die."

"You watched my *body* die. A lifeless husk. My soul took possession of John Wilkes Booth the night before; when the bastard visited me, asking if he could study me for a play he was planning to write."

"Impossible!" Stanton exclaimed. "I would have known!"

"Do you think you are aware of every one of the Gifted?" John Brown asked.

"Yes. We have mediums who…"

"Mediums?" Brown growled. "I *become* whoever I possess, fool. Their memories…their skills and talents…all mine."

He paced around his cell. "When I return to my body…well, when I *had* a body, my host has no recollection of the possession. So your mediums are no good against me."

"But why, John?" Harriet asked. "We were friends!"

"Friends?" he hissed. "You left me to *die* at Harper's Ferry!"

Brown grabbed the bars and sneered at Harriet. "*You* were the one who the Negroes rallied around. If you had been there, an *army* would have been at my back. This world would be *ours*!"

"The Lawd showed me the truth, John," Harriet replied. "You would have turned this world into Hell. Us Negroes would have still been slaves, with just *one* slave master…you."

"You lying *bitch*!" He shouted.

"I speak the truth, John," Harriet said. "Ben is a slave to you right now. Set him free. Your quarrel ain't with him."

He laughed. "I am going to make your nephew famous, Harriet. Where Nat Turner failed, Ben will succeed. I am going to bathe this country in white blood! And Negroes will rally behind 'Ben Ross, kin of the great General Harriet Tubman'!"

"You are a bit late, Booth…or Brown…or who*ever* in the hell you are. Lincoln already *freed* the Negroes," Stanton said.

"You are truly a fool!" John Brown shot back. "Lincoln *emancipated* the slaves. Instead of the Negroes being *private* property, they are now property of the United States of America: a country that considers them only three-fifths of a human being."

He smiled at Stanton and licked his lips. "So, if your secret gets out, it's back to the plantation for *you*, Mr. Secretary!"

Druga struggled to sit up. She clutched at her chest, as her broken ribs grated against her lungs."Your *mother?"* She gasped.

Stanton exchanged a quick glance with Mama Maybelle. "Yes, my mother was a Negro," But she was *never* a slave."

"Any Negro who walks the cursed soil of America is a slave – no matter how free they believe themselves to be!" Brown sneered. "I am going to change that!"

The door to the jail flung open. Everyone sat quietly, waiting to see who would come down the short flight of stairs to the detention area. The Captain who had taken them captive entered.

"Good afternoon amigos," he said. "My name is Captain Jaime Vega."

Captain Vega approached "Ben's" cell, but paused and looked over his shoulder at Stanton. "Your identity has been confirmed. After I take your statement, you and your…operatives are free to go."

"Where is my daughter?" Stanton asked.

"She is at my home, just up the hill," Captain Vega answered. "My wife and daughter are taking good care of her. I will take you to her soon."

"And what of Harriet and her nephew, Ben," Stanton asked; staring at the ersatz Ben with contempt.

Captain Vega opened "Ben's" cell and pulled him out. "They shall remain here until Pinkertons arrives to return them to San Antonio. It appears they are wanted for murder."

"Murder?" Harriet inquired.

"I can't go on lyin,' Aunt Harriet," John Brown cried. "I'm going to sign a confession. We can't go on killin' these good white folks like this, Auntie!"

Harriet clenched her fists. Her breathing grew shallow and her jaw tightened. "I'm gon' set you free, Ben – I promise!"

"Only the truth gon' set *me* free, Auntie," John Brown said with a sly smile.

Suddenly, a soldier stumbled into the detention area and collapsed at Captain Vega's feet.

"Madre de Dios!" Captain Vega said, as he crouched down to examine the soldier.

Corporal Manuel Alejandro Rivera's skin was on fire. Captain Vega cradled the Corporal's head in his arms and studied his face.

What the Captain saw frightened him.

Corporal Rivera was decomposing.

His skin had turned a greenish-gray hue, and was cracking open in places. His eyes were sunken and dull. And his lips were beginning to recede: revealing cracked and jagged teeth.

Stanton caught a glimpse of the Corporal. "Oh, *no!*" he whispered.

"What happened to you, soldier?" Captain Vega asked.

"It came for me at the infirmary," Corporal Rivera whispered hoarsely. "And then... it took the men. One, by one."

"Your skin is so hot! You're delirious from fever!"

"Kill him Captain!" Stanton screamed. "He is infected! Kill him now!"

Captain Vega looked up at Stanton. The Secretary of War's terrified expression perplexed him. "What...?"

Corporal Rivera sprang upwards and sank his teeth into Captain Vega's throat.

Blood gurgled up in the Captain's mouth and spilled from between his lips.

John Brown turned to Harriet and smiled. "See you soon!"

He sprinted up the stairs and out of the jail, chuckling as the noonday sun embraced him.

Stanton backed away, towards the rear of his cell, as he watched Corporal Rivera gnaw at Captain Vega's esophagus. "Mama Maybelle, get us out of here!"

Maybelle grabbed the bars. "About time! What's going on child? What's wrong with that boy eatin' away at the Captain?"

"It's Caleb!" Stanton answered, his eyes still on Rivera. "I infected him, but I did not have the opportunity to kill him! He is now a *ghul!*"

"A ghul?" Druga inquired.

"Yes...a creature that eats *human* flesh to halt the decay of its *own*. The condition is highly contagious. I carry the disease in my body fluids, but I do not suffer its effects."

Corporal Rivera was now cheerfully chewing off Captain Vega's face.

"But your wife – ?" Druga began.

"Is immune," Stanton said, interrupting her. "My wife is one of the Gifted. She is immune to all poisons and contagion – one of the reasons I married her."

Mama Maybelle tore the door of her cell out of the floor and ceiling, and then hurled it at Corporal Rivera. The heavy iron door rent the Corporal's decaying body in half. Captain Vega fell to the floor of the detention area. Blood continued to flow from his gaping neck and formed a crimson halo around his head.

The door lodged in the wall about six inches.

Mama Maybelle stood over Captain Vega. His face was already beginning to turn a pallid green. She raised her knee to her rotund belly and then slammed her heavy leg down, smashing the Captain's head under her plump foot.

"Now, *us* please," Stanton said. "Druga first."

"Of course, child," Mama Maybelle replied, as she lifted Druga onto her haunches.

Druga scooted out of the cell. She winced from the pain in her side.

"Hold on, child," Mama Maybelle said to Druga. "As soon as we get home, I'll take you to a healer friend o' mine; and he will fix you right up."

"That he will!" Stanton agreed. "Now if you will, please hurry! If Caleb is on the loose out there, this whole fort may be overrun with ghuls! I have to get to Margaret now!"

Mama Maybelle went to Stanton's cell and pulled with a mighty heave. The locking mechanism exploded. Bolts, screws and metal plates rained upon the floor. Stanton quickly exited his cell and briskly walked toward the stairs.

"What about her?" Druga asked, pointing toward Harriet's cell.

"Leave her," Stanton replied. "She *caused* all this by kidnapping my Margaret, and bringing her to this God-forsaken place."

"I was only doin' what the Lawd told me to do," Harriet said.

Stanton looked over his shoulder at her and smirked. "Then, I am sure the *Lord* shall set you free."

He ran up the stairs and pushed the door open. Light from the afternoon sun chased away the shadows in the holding cells. The Secretary of War left the jail and the hunters followed him, letting the door slam behind them.

And the shadows returned.

CHAPTER 35

May 1, 1865

Hell had come to Fort Milagros.

Half-consumed bodies, tattered limbs, festering entrails…were strewn throughout the streets…upon the rooftops…hanging from fence-posts and clotheslines. Half of the inhabitants of Fort Milagros were dead. The other half had succumbed to the infection and were now ghuls.

The decomposing Children of Caleb.

"Damn!" Stanton sighed.

"The *damned* is more like it," Druga said.

A shift in the corner of the Russian huntress' eye caught her attention. She snapped her head toward the movement and – for the first time in her life – was afraid. *"Look!* At your nine o'clock!"

Stanton and Mama Maybelle turned to face what had alarmed Druga so.

"Gods help us!" Mama Maybelle whispered.

An army stood before them. An army unlike the world had ever seen.

Some of the soldiers looked like four-legged man-spiders – their rotting limbs freakishly elongated and bent at harsh angles. Others resembled putrescent snakes. And some had fused together, forming what looked like a giant centipede, standing upright.

Standing at the front of the army of ghuls, was their general: Caleb Butler.

Caleb smiled at Stanton and looked down between his legs at his prize: Margaret.

He gently ran his skeletal right hand through Margaret's hair. His left hand lay on her heaving chest. His middle finger – now stretched to twice its normal length, with a razor sharp claw protruding from the bony digit – tapped at her throat. Margaret sobbed weakly.

"Let her go, Caleb!" Stanton pleaded. "Your quarrel is with me, not the child!"

"We got no quarrel, Stanton," Caleb replied. "Shoot, if anything, you made me…*better*."

"Give the girl to me, Caleb. *Please.*"

"Tell me where Harriet is," Caleb ran his finger gently across Margaret's throat. "Now, if she's dead or if you lie, in regards to her whereabouts, I'll open this little angel up. Understand?"

Stanton closed his eyes and nodded. "We left her locked up in the jail."

Caleb laughed. "You are a cold-hearted bastard, Stanton!"

The Commander of the ghul army turned to one of the spider-creatures. "Go check! But don't hurt her!"

The ghul scurried off toward the jail.

Caleb returned his attention to Stanton, and stared at the Secretary of War – unblinking – with a wide grin upon his decomposing face.

A few moments later, the man-spider returned.

"Well?" Caleb inquired. The creature nodded.

Caleb shoved Margaret toward Stanton. Stanton pulled her to him and held her tightly. Caleb addressed his army. "To the jail!"

The ghuls charged toward the jail, and he turned to Stanton. "Do *not* be here when we return!"

Caleb grinned, tilted his hat and sprinted toward the jailhouse.

Stanton hugged Margaret, and planted kisses on her forehead and cheeks. "My *baby!* My precious, little princess!"

Mama Maybelle wiped a tear from her cheek and smiled. She placed a firm hand upon Stanton's shoulder. "We have to go, child. Those things looked hungry, and Mama makes more than a morsel, so…"

Stanton grabbed Margaret's hand and stood up. "Of course." He quickly scanned the area until he found what he was searching for. He pointed toward the stables. "Over there... a wagon."

Mama Maybelle wrapped Druga and Stanton in her thick arms. Stanton held Margaret to his chest.

The giantess bent her knees deeply, and then sprang upward – her powerful leap propelling them toward the wagon. She landed with a booming thud. The ground shook, and a cloud of sand rose to the heavens.

Stanton hoisted Margaret into the back of the wagon. Druga climbed inside and lay on her back to give rest to her aching ribs. The wagon's undercarriage sank an inch closer to its wheels as Mama Maybelle climbed into it.

"I'll drive!" Stanton said. "We need to get as far away from this damnable place as possible – and with great haste!"

The wagon sped away, leaving Hell behind.

CHAPTER 36

May 1, 1865

When the spider-ghul burst into the jail, peeked in her cell and rushed out as quickly as it came in; Harriet knew her condition was about to become dire.

She knelt at the back of her cell, bowed her head and began to pray. "Lawd, I came here 'cause you commanded it to be so. In my ign'ance, I thought it was to reunite that baby with her daddy, but that was just a small part, wasn't it, Lawd?"

The rumbling of many feet pounding the desert sand drew nearer to the jail.

Harriet slowed her breathing and relaxed. She continued to pray. "The forces of Hell have been let loose, and you done led them here to stop them."

The door to the jail flung open. The smell of stale blood and fetid meat rushed in.

"Lawd," Harriet continued. "Bless me to carry on your work for just a li'l while longer. Make me a shackle about Satan's ankle, Lawd."

The sound of boots striking stone echoed in the stairway.

Harriet continued to pray. "Your enemies descend upon me, Father. Let me…"

A searing pain in Harriet's chest shut her mouth. She searched for the source of her agony and found Caleb's hand – the ossiferous fingers elongated and fused into a spear – protruding from her sternum.

Caleb yanked his hand from Harriet's chest, leaving a gaping hole. "*That's* for my brother!" She crumpled onto the floor.

He dipped his fingers into the mess that was once Captain Vega and withdrew a ring of keys. “Now it’s time for my afternoon snack…and I just *love* dark meat!”

Harriet crawled to the back of her cell. A trail of blood followed her.

Caleb laughed. “You have nowhere to go, Harriet Tubman.” He unlocked the door and stepped into her cell. “After I’m done with you, my soldiers will pick your bones clean.”

He squatted down over Harriet and straddled her waist with his knees. “God, I bet you’d go great with a pot of pinto beans!”

Caleb licked his lips obscenely. He was hungry and about to be well fed.

CHAPTER 37

May 1, 1865

"Those things, ghuls you called them, they are all so…diverse." Druga said as she climbed out of the wagon.

"The germ changes once it finds a host," Stanton replied. "So, no two ghuls are alike. But they all die the same – by destroying the brain or by starving them to death."

"Starving them?" Druga asked.

"Yes, it usually takes about a day and a half. They have to eat a few pounds of human flesh a day, to stop the rapid decomposition caused by the infection."

"And Caleb? The other ghuls seem to follow his lead."

"Yes, that concerns me," Stanton said. "I have created a dozen ghuls for study; and none of them exhibited anything other than basic survival instincts and animal-like cunning. *Never* have they been organized, nor have they followed another before. I assume it has something to do with Caleb being one of the Gifted."

Margaret laid her head on Mama Maybelle's lap and covered her ears. "I don't want to hear anymore, daddy!"

The giantess placed a soft, plump hand on Margaret's forehead. "This child is burning up! Her skin is like fire!"

Stanton ran to Mama Maybelle's side and crouched beside her. He placed the back of his hand on Margaret's neck. Though her neck was burning hot, it gave Stanton chills.

"No!" he whispered.

Frantic, Stanton nervously inspected Margaret's skin. Finally, he found it behind her knee: a tiny break in the flesh.

"Did anyone, or any*thing*, hurt you, Margaret?"

“When I first saw that man with the funny hands, I tried to run! But he grabbed me by the leg! I got scratched daddy. But then the man put some of his spit on it and made it feel better.”

Stanton felt weak. Dizzy. He placed his hand against Mama Maybelle’s shoulder to steady himself. “My baby...My poor baby!”

He stood and hopped back in the driver’s seat of the wagon. “We have to go back to Fort Milagros!”

“Why?” Druga asked.

“Harriet heals rapidly!” Stanton answered. “Her bones – her blood. If we can give Harriet’s blood to Margaret, we may be able to prevent the virus from taking her; or even reverse its effects.”

“How much blood will she need?” Mama Maybelle inquired.

“I have no idea,” Stanton replied. We’ll just have to take it all.”

“Then we better move fast! And let’s pray there’s something left of Harriet when we get there!”

CHAPTER 38

May 1, 1865

Caleb sank his teeth into Harriet's throat.

The salty sweetness of Harriet's blood was not his reward, however. Only the unpleasant taste of duck feathers and dirty cotton.

The cell door slammed shut and clicked as the lock engaged.

The illusion faded.

Harriet was not beneath Caleb. He was straddling a filthy mattress, which he had torn into with his jagged teeth. Feathers flew all over the cell. He screamed as he tossed the mattress aside.

Harriet crawled toward Captain Vega's revolver.

The ghul rolled toward the bars of the cell, and thrust his hand between them. His fingers elongated into thin tentacles that lashed out at Harriet.

The bone-tentacles wrapped around Harriet's ankle.

Caleb willed the tentacles to shorten. Harriet slid across the floor, back toward his other hand, which was formed into the shape of a wicked-looking, alabaster axe.

Harriet rolled onto her back and fired the revolver.

Blood painted the rear wall of the cell.

Caleb fell onto his back. His fingers released Harriet's ankle and shrank to their normal length. The General of the ghul Army lay still. Smoke rose from the hole in the center of his forehead.

Harriet quickly crawled to the stairs and dragged herself up to the door. She struggled to her feet and locked it. She knew the ghuls would come, once they figured out that their master had not done the shooting.

Blood continued to flow from the hole in Harriet's chest. She fought back the darkness that threatened to overcome her, and stumbled back down the stairs. She leaned against her former cell, and pulled the keys from the lock.

The ghuls began pounding on the door.

Harriet made her way back up the stairs and to the storage closet. She tried to turn the knob. The door was locked. She fumbled with the keys, trying different ones until – finally – she found the key that unlocked the door.

Inside the closet were more shackles, a broom; and a crate filled with items that once belonged to former guests of the jail. Harriet removed her bandana, and pressed it against the wound in her chest. She then used her free hand to quickly clear everything from the closet.

Harriet crawled inside.

She squeezed the keys between her fingers, making a spiked mace of her fist and began punching the lime mortar between the bricks that comprised the rear closet wall.

The mortar cracked and fell – in flakes – on the floor of the closet.

The jail door shuddered.

Harriet heard a loud cracking noise behind her. It sounded as if the ghuls were pounding the iron door off its hinges. She ignored the pain in her chest and punched the wall even harder.

A brick fell from the wall...then another...and another. Light from the afternoon sun poured in.

The jail door flew off its hinges and the ghuls scurried, shambled and shuffled inside.

Harriet closed the closet door and then rammed the wall with her shoulder. The wall collapsed and she fell into the light. She quickly crawled away from the jail and across the sea of entrails, bone and skin toward the stables.

The ghul soldiers piled into the jail and down to the detention area... where they found their fallen general.

The creatures examined Caleb with curiosity and confusion.

Something under Caleb's shirt rolled…shifted…pulsed. His body jerked and his hips rose and fell violently…and then he fell still again. A moment later, his hands clawed at his shirt and then ripped it open. His eyes, however, remained lifeless.

Caleb tore the shirt to shreds, exposing his upper body completely.

Seemingly carved into Caleb's torso, was a raised sculpture of his face.

Suddenly, the eyes of the face sprang open and the mouth formed a wide grin.

The General of the ghuls sat upright. His lifeless head flopped around on his neck like a trout on dry land. But the face in his torso was alert, its eyes perusing the soldiers standing before him.

"Find the keys and get me out of here!" Caleb's torso commanded. "We got some killin' to do!"

CHAPTER 39

May 1, 1865

Fort Milagros was quiet.

"Stay alert," Stanton whispered. "This might be a trap."

"No, no trap," Druga said, sniffing the warm, dry, evening air. "Everyone is gone."

"What about Harriet?" Stanton asked. "Is she…"

"Alive," Druga replied. "But, she, too, is gone."

"Damn it! Which way?"

Druga walked around their wagon, sniffing the air. "North...the ghuls have gone in the same direction."

"North it is, then!" Stanton said.

He walked around to the back of the wagon. Mama Maybelle was standing there, wiping tears from her eyes

"How is Margaret?" the Secretary of War asked.

They peeked into the wagon. Margaret strained against the ropes Maybelle had tied around her wrists and ankles.

The little girl's skin had turned a pallid gray-green. Her eyes were sunken and dark, but they burned with rage…and hunger.

"Change the horses, child!" Mama Maybelle said. "We gon' have to run 'em into the ground!"

CHAPTER 40

May 2, 1865

Punta Blanca would never be the same. Its leader and only Man of-the-Cloth, Father Ramon, was dying.

Harriet walked into the church's rectory. Father Ramon lay on his bed. Blood seeped from several slashes and puncture wounds, throughout the priest's body.

Three women attended to his wounds as they chanted prayers and incantations in Spanish, Latin. It was a tongue that Harriet had never heard before, but it sounded as old as the Mexican pyramids themselves.

"Harriet," Father Ramon coughed, as he weakly extended a hand toward her.

The priest's hand went limp and Harriet caught it in hers. "What happened, Padre?"

Father Ramon lowered his gaze. "It was Ben, Harriet. He came to me this morning, confessing to have been coerced by Edwin Stanton to betray you. He said he wanted to make amends. He sounded so…sincere."

The priest convulsed as he coughed up a clot of blood. He shut his eyes and inhaled deeply. The women around his bed prayed and chanted frantically, splashing holy water on the priest's forehead. The convulsion subsided.

Father Ramon squeezed Harriet's hand. "He said he wanted to make amends. I gave him a change of clothes…food…water. While I was praying for Ben, he attacked."

"Lawd," She sighed.

Father Ramon's body stiffened and his eyes glazed over. "Harriet…I…I can't see you."

Harriet kissed him on the forehead. "Lawd, take your son into your bosom. Forgive him of any sin, and welcome him into your army of Angels, Lawd. Amen."

Father Ramon's grip on Harriet's hand loosened and his body went limp. She placed the priest's hand on his chest and rose from the bed.

Harriet turned to leave the room, but paused in the doorway. "Sisters?"

"Si?" The Elder Nun replied.

"I won't bother you for much, but I'll be needin' a gun and a rifle."

"Si."

The Elder Sister stared into Father Ramon's lifeless eyes. "And what will you do when you find the man, who did this to Father Ramon? He is your nephew, si?"

Harriet's eyes were hard. *"Look* like ain't always *be*, sister," she said. "When I find Ben, I'm gon' drive the evil out that's in him! And send it back to Hell, where it belongs!"

BOOK 2: JUDGES

CHAPTER 41

May 3, 1865

Harriet parted the dingy, white lace curtains and studied the villagers as they marched – with heads hung low – in a long queue toward the church.

They would bury Father Ramon today and – if the Lawd saw fit to let Harriet have her way – she would bury John Brown today also.

Harriet turned away from the window and resumed her search of Sinai's cabin.

Argentine blades and bullets, used for killing lycanthropes, were in abundance; as were stakes of sharpened oak; and axes and swords of cold steel – common tools of the trade of one who hunts monsters.

Inside a silver box, tucked under Sinai's bed, Harriet found what she was looking for – the *Bello Mule* – a .48 caliber revolver that possessed two barrels and a drum-like cylinder, with twenty chambers arranged in two rows – a monstrous weapon with which to fight monstrous foes.

Baas had given *the Mule* to Sinai for his birthday a decade ago. The old monster-hunter had put the weapon to use many times.

"Lawd, let me wield this half as good as old Sinai and I'll be satisfied," Harriet whispered, slipping the *Bello Mule* into its massive, leather holster, which she now wore strapped across her chest.

Harriet scooped several fistfuls of silver .48 caliber bullets from the box that housed *the Mule* and tossed them into leather pouches on the belt she had secured around her waist over her charcoal-gray, cotton blouse.

She stepped out of the hot shadows of the house into the cool breeze that blew across the oasis in the desert that was the village of Punta Blanca.

The warrior woman hopped into Sinai's cart and inspected its contents to ensure she had not forgotten anything important during her hasty packing of the vehicle. "Two shotguns…crate of buckshot…bag of jerky…barrel of water…I don't think we missed nothin', Lawd, so I'll be takin' my leave now. I 'magine you'll be showin' me John Brown's whereabouts soon, Lawd and – as promised – I'll be sendin' him on down to perdition, where he belong."

Harriet looked toward the horizon. A large dust cloud rolled toward the village. Harriet reached inside her overcoat and withdrew her goggles. She slipped them onto her face. The bronze and leather eyewear cooled her cocoa skin.

And then the world tumbled…tilted…fell...whirling around Harriet like a maelstrom, filled with ire and spite.

A giant human skeleton, with two snarling heads, burst from the spinning chaos and landed before Harriet.

The monstrous relic sported a cape fashioned from dirt and a sword forged from the putrid corpses of Mexican *soldados* – the plumed helmeted soldiers Harriet faced three days earlier, in Punta Blanca. The skeleton's heads laughed and then the creature slashed toward Harriet's neck with its corpse-sword.

The whirling of the world stopped.

Harriet rose from the floor of the cart and hopped into the drivers' seat. "Yah," she shouted, snapping the reins she clutched in her fists. The twin horses bolted toward the church.

"Your guns!" Harriet screamed. "Get your guns an' get ready!"

The villagers turned toward Harriet with puzzled expressions.

"Get ready for what?" A nun asked.

Harriet pointed toward the cloud of dirt rolling toward them. "Hell."

****

"Enjoy the fiesta, amigos, but save Harriet for *me*!" Caleb commanded, as the horde of ghuls charged toward the church.

Caleb's lifeless head bounced from side-to-side as the spider-ghul upon whose back he rode, galloped nimbly upon its gangly, elongated arms and legs. The face etched into Caleb's torso grinned sardonically. "Nowhere to run now, Moses. Nowhere to run!"

****

The villagers leapt into action, darting about like a hive of honeybees, as they prepared for battle.

The small children were ushered into the church, guarded by shotgun wielding elders and women in the latter stages of pregnancy.

The rest of the villagers took cover behind water-barrels and fruit carts; on the sides of houses and shops and on the roof of the church.

Harriet knelt in the back of Sinai's cart and jerked the *Bello Mule* from its holster. She lifted the heavy weapon and pointed its twin barrels toward the dust cloud.

"Fire!" Harriet shouted as she squeezed *the Mule*'s trigger.

A loud din – accompanied by a flash of fire – erupted from the *Bello Mule*'s dual muzzles and the thunderous roar of a hundred exploding rifles and shotguns tore the sky asunder.

A moment later, a hair-raising wail rose from the dust cloud as scores of ghuls fell.

"And I heard – as it were – the noise of thunder," the Elder Sister uttered. "And one of the four beasts said 'come and see'; and I saw…"

The ghul-horde descended upon the village.

Cries of fear and disgust rose from the villagers as they got a clear view of the monstrous army of living dead.

Harriet perused the horde and spotted Caleb amidst his putrid brethren. She aimed the *Bello Mule* at the smiling face in his torso. "And I beheld a pale horse, whose rider was Death; and Hell followed with him."

Harriet fired again. Two powerful rounds burst from the barrels of the weapon and sped toward Caleb's chest.

Suddenly, the spider-ghul Caleb rode upon leapt upward, rising high above the horde and taking Caleb out of the line of fire.

The pair of bullets struck the spider-ghul in the lower abdomen.

The creature loosed a shrill cry as the lower half of its body was rent from its torso.

Caleb was sent flying as the spider-ghul's torn body fell to the earth, landing in two mangled piles of rot.

Caleb tumbled head-over-heels, stopping – with a loud crack – as his back slammed into the stable.

"Fire!" Harriet shouted once more.

In unison, the villagers fired upon the Ghul Army a second time. A mass of monstrosities fell under the storm of iron and silver. There was a multitude more, however, and – in one frightening wave of brutal retaliation – the villagers were nearly completely decimated.

Yet, the stalwart inhabitants of Punta Blanca fought on, inspirited by Harriet Tubman and the souls of their fallen comrades.

The air reeked of gunpowder, blood and putrefaction, but Harriet could still detect the foul stench of the ghuls' general as he crept toward her right flank.

She snapped her head to her right and met Caleb's wicked gaze with a powerful stare of her own.

"Harriet Tubman," Caleb hissed. "You and me – we gotta have us a little pow-wow."

"I think I'll let this here iron do the talking for me," Harriet replied, brandishing the *Bello Mule*.

Caleb's torso-face grinned wickedly. "Aw, come on, Harriet; I got something I wanna get off my chest!" Caleb's lifeless head bounced back and forth on his rubbery neck as the monster laughed at the pun.

"I reckon *I* can remove it for you."

Harriet fired the *Bello Mule*.

Caleb leapt to his left, but he wasn't quite fast enough and both rounds struck home, tearing out the right corner of his "mouth".

The General of the Ghul Army roared as he rolled around on the ground in agony.

The ghul-horde charged Harriet's cart, swarming it like ants on a crust of bread.

"Through you, Lawd, I will push down my enemies," Harriet shouted, unleashing volley after volley of searing metal from the *Bello Mule*. "Through your name, I will trample those who rise up against me!"

A sticky, greenish-black ichor rose from amidst the horde as dozens of the creatures fell.

The Ghul Army's numbers were too great, however, and within moments, the cart was overrun and Harriet was overrun. Clawed hands clutched at her ankles; spindly arms encircled her waist and neck. Harriet was snatched from the cart and pulled toward certain death.

"I'll be shaking hands with you shortly, Lawd," Harriet said. "Please, save a spot for me in your Army of Angels, Father, so I can keep on fightin' the good fight!"

Suddenly, a thunderous din rose from the earth. An instant later, Harriet – and the ghuls that held her in their grasp – were propelled into the air by a powerful wave of force that erupted from beneath their feet. Harriet rolled with the force, somersaulting backward and landing upon one knee.

"*Your Lord is gonna have to wait on that handshake, child.*"

Harriet looked up toward the strong, alto voice.

Standing before her was the giantess, Mama Maybelle.

The ebon-skinned colossus pulled Harriet to her feet and then wrapped a massive arm around her.

"Stop her!" Caleb screamed, struggling to his knees.

The horde surged toward Mama Maybelle.

The giantess coiled her densely muscled back, bent her knees deeply and then exploded upward, leaping high into the air. Mama Maybelle etched a wide arc across the sky as the mighty leap sped them away from the screaming horde of ghuls.

The breeze upon Harriet's face invigorated her…and made her painfully aware of whose cargo she was. Her index finger crept toward the trigger of the *Bello Mule*.

"Touch that trigger and Mama will tear your head off, child," Mama Maybelle crooned as she descended upon a patch of grass.

Harriet holstered *the Mule*.

A covered wagon sped toward them, it wheels rumbling loudly as they rolled across the uneven plain.

The rumbling of the wheels could not, however, drown out the roar of the Ghul Army, which grew louder with each passing second.

The wagon came to a stop in front of Harriet. Edwin Stanton sat in the driver's seat.

"They closing on us fast, child," Mama Maybelle said as she trotted toward the back of the wagon. "We have to go now!"

"Sit up here with me, Harriet," the Secretary of War said, offering his hand to help her up.

Harriet did not budge.

"Please," Stanton sighed. "We have little time. Those monsters will be on us soon."

Harriet pushed Stanton's hand aside and leapt up into the seat beside him.

The wagon creaked in protest as Mama Maybelle climbed into the back of it.

Stanton snapped the reigns and the horses broke into a gallop. The wagon sped away, leaving the carnage at Punta Blanca far behind it.

CHAPTER 42

May 3, 1865

"So, why did y'all save me from those demons back there?" Harriet asked, resting her hand on the copper grip of the *Bello Mule*.

"The Lord works in mysterious ways, does He not?" Stanton replied.

"Yeah," Harriet said. "Question is…is this the *Lawd's* work, or the labor of somethin' *else*?"

"In his great 'Sermon on the Mount', did not the Lord say 'Love your enemies, bless them that curse you, do good to them that hate you, and pray for them which despitefully use you and persecute you?" Stanton asked.

"Yes, He did," Harriet answered. "But, I think it was in that same sermon that the Lawd said 'Many will say to me in that day, Lawd, have we not prophesied in thy name? And in thy name, have cast out devils? And in thy name, have done many wonderful works? And then will I profess unto them, I never knew you; depart from me, ye that work iniquity."

"Touché, Harriet," Stanton said, shaking his head. "But did not the Lord also say do the…unto him that…oh, hell…Mama Maybelle!"

A massive fist shot out from the cart and hammered into the back of Harriet's neck.

Her body went limp and slumped forward in her seat.

"You didn't kill her, did you?" Stanton inquired.

"No, child," Maybelle answered. "With her healing abilities, that broken neck should heal up in no time. It'll take a couple of days for her brain to sort itself out. She'll sleep 'til then."

"Excellent," Stanton said, smiling. "More than enough time!"

"We must move quickly, comrades," Druga said. "The little one smells…different."

"Hang on, child," Mama Maybelle said, rubbing Margaret's moist, pallid forehead. "We'll have you right as rain in just a little bit."

Margaret answered with a low growl and a hungry stare.

CHAPTER 43

May 5, 1865

"Do you really think she is playing possum, Druga?" Stanton asked, lighting the tip of a large cigar. "Mama Maybelle hit her pretty hard."

"I *know* she is," Druga replied. "Her heartbeat…her smell…she is awake."

"*There is one way we can find out, oui*?" An unfamiliar voice said. The man's voice was a silky tenor, which accentuated his French accent. "*I will climb up here and have my way with her. You are welcome to watch if you'd like.*"

Harriet's eyes popped open. "They will be watchin' you die a painful death if you do."

"Ah, Mademoiselle Tubman, you *are* awake," the man snickered. "I am Dr. Louis Pasteur and I am quite pleased to make your acquaintance."

"You normally chain your patients to their beds, doctor?" Harriet asked as she yanked the heavy chains that bound her ankles and wrists to the bedrails.

"Non, not normally," Dr. Pasteur said. "However, you are far from normal, oui?"

"Why you doin' this, Mr. Secretary?" Harriet asked, turning her head toward Stanton who loomed over her.

"Margaret is…not well," Stanton replied. "She needs your blood, Harriet, or she will be lost to me forever."

"She gon' drink my blood? She a vampire now?"

Stanton nodded toward something to Harriet's right. "Worse."

Harriet turned her head. Lying in a bed beside her was a rapidly breathing Margaret. The child's bloodshot eyes rolled wildly in their sockets and her mouth – tilted at an impossible upward angle toward the right side of her face – was locked in a salivating grin.

"Lawd," Harriet sighed.

"She was infected by Caleb Butler," Stanton said.

"The cowboy," Harriet replied.

"Yes," Stanton said. "I believe the healing properties of your blood can cure her. I have hired Dr. Pasteur to do a procedure called a blood transfusion. Dr. Pasteur?"

"Basically, we are going to replace Margaret's diseased blood with about three quarters of *your* blood."

"I would have given that to the child freely," Harriet said. "You know that, Secretary Stanton, so, why almost kill me by breaking my neck? Why the chains?"

"*Because he has promised the remainder of your blood to me.*"

Harriet snapped her head to the left – toward the familiar voice. Druga Minkoff lay in a bed identical to Margaret's. Her face was a mask of pain.

Harriet returned her attention to Edwin Stanton. "Do your worst, then; if the Lawd see fit, we gon' settle up after and I promise to repay you in kind."

"I believe you will certainly try," Stanton replied. "Dr. Pasteur, please, proceed."

CHAPTER 44

May 5, 1865

The Nefertiti sped across the clear, Northwestern sky.

"Forgive me, Harriet," Baas Bello whispered as he unfolded a piece of paper that lay in his lap. "But I must follow this lead on The Alchemist – or , more accurately, Professor Amschel Kleinhopper."

Baas studied the piece of paper – a flyer publicizing 'Kleinhopper's Karnival of Konstructs' – at the center of which was a photo…of a *knoll* – the wicked creature that had taken Baas' beloved son-in-law, Talltrees, forever from this world.

The flyer said the Karnival would take place in New Orleans on May 7, 1865. In two days. Two days from Baas avenging Talltrees' death.

Baas had discovered the flyer the day before, after his pass over the rendezvous point where Harriet agreed to meet him once her mission in Mexico was resolved. Harriet was not there. Baas had flown into Galveston, Texas for supplies, where he discovered the flyer in one of the stores owned by Harley Boyd – owner of several supply depots throughout the United States and former conductor on the Underground Railroad.

And now, he was flying to the Nebraska Territory to enlist the aid of the only person, besides Harriet Tubman, he believed he could take into battle against Professor Kleinhopper and his constructs and they both come out alive.

"Black Mary," Baas sighed. "Here I come."

CHAPTER 45

May 5, 1865

Harriet's skin had gone pale…cold. She was too weak to even open her eyes and the voices in the room sounded muffled and faded in and out.

"Margaret looks…temporary…she will…her mind, oui?"

"…blood…Harriet…die…immortal?...kill us all…reinforce chains!"

"…life, child…Mama will rip…Caleb…Auburn."

Slowly, she felt the strength creep back into her muscles and deep in the marrow of her bones. Harriet focused on the voices in the room and they became clearer by the second.

"Dr. Pasteur, we are going to take Margaret to a safe-house in the French Quarter," Edwin Stanton said. "We will return for Druga in the morning."

"Magnifique, Monsieur Stanton," the doctor replied. "Per your instructions, after the transfusion is complete, I will remove Harriet's organs and pack them on ice for you."

"Very good," Stanton said with a tip of his top-hat. "Godspeed, Druga."

Das vedanya," Druga replied, smiling weakly. Her metallic fangs reflected the sun's rays, which shone through the ceiling's skylight, making her look, at once, vulnerable and sinister.

Stanton shoved a huge Prominente cigar between his lips and then sauntered out of the room. Mama Maybelle followed him, with Margaret cradled, like a newborn baby, in her massive arms.

Dr. Pasteur turned to Druga and gently grabbed her right wrist. He strapped her arm to the bedrail and then moved down toward her ankle.

"Are these restraints necessary?" Druga asked.

"Oui," Dr. Pasteur answered. "We do not know how you will react to Mademoiselle Tubman's blood, so we must keep you immobilized so you do not injure yourself."

Druga nodded in approval.

Dr. Pasteur strapped her right ankle and then repeated the process on the Russian assassin's left side. "Now, for the transfusion of the blood."

Harriet felt a sudden burst of power as blood rushed into her veins.

"Doctor," Druga cried. "Something is wrong. I feel…weak. I…"

"You are *dying*, you idiot," Doctor Pasteur said, interrupting her. "Now, shut up and *do* it; your accent annoys me!"

Druga's mouth fell slack. "What?"

"I am not giving *you* Harriet's blood, woman," Dr. Pasteur replied. "I am giving *your* blood to *her*."

"But, why?"

"Because I need her alive; to rot in prison and to serve as inspiration for the coming revolution, when the slave takes this land from his master!"

"John Brown," Harriet whispered.

"Oui, General Tubman," John Brown replied. "Do you like this new body of mine?"

"Where's Ben?" Harriet asked.

"He's somewhere safe," John Brown replied. "Don't worry, I won't hurt him. I need Ben to become the face of the coming revolution."

Druga convulsed as her life's essence was sucked from her veins. Her flesh turned a dull alabaster and the shine quickly faded from her eyes.

"The Russian will be dead in a few seconds," John Brown said, unlocking the padlocks that secured the chains wrapped around

Harriet's wrists and ankles. "And in a minute or two, you'll be strong enough to get up from that table and do me harm; so, I must now take my leave and take possession of an eloquent negro, who shall plead your case and make you the 'mother of the movement'."

"Frederick!" Harriet gasped. "You plan to take poor Frederick Douglass as your next victim!"

Dr. Louis Pasteur's face smiled John Brown's wicked smile. "Au revoir, Harriet."

John Brown briskly exited the room.

Harriet was a blur, rapidly shaking her hands and feet to unravel the chains that bound her and then leapt from the table and sprinted toward the door, pausing to glance at Druga's emaciated husk.

Satisfied that Druga would never again hurt her, or anyone else, she darted out of the room.

In contrast to the pristine whiteness of the operating room behind Harriet, the large room she stepped into was constructed of red brick, with a dusty, hardwood floor. The room was empty, save for a bronze table with four matching bronze chairs.

Harriet ran to the door and kicked it open.

She was greeted by cobblestone streets; shops of Spanish and French design; and the smell of coffee pastries and fresh bread.

Harriet recognized her surroundings. She had been here many times before.

"New Orleans, she said, shaking her head. "Lawd, I need transportation…and weapons; I reckon I got to go see Madame d'Oliva."

CHAPTER 46

May 5, 1865

The Nebraska territory was wild; rough; violent…and Mary Fields – 'Black Mary' – seemed the embodiment of this hard, harsh land.

Mary sat upon a patch of grass, devouring a jar of pinto beans. Several empty jars lay scattered, in a semi-circle, before her.

After finishing off the last can, the statuesque woman grabbed her Sharp's carbine with one large, mahogany hand and a half-consumed bottle of whiskey with the other.

Mary laid the carbine in her lap and pressed the opening of the bottle to her full lips. She turned the bottle upside down, allowing the ardent spirits to flow – in hot rivers – down her gullet and into her gut.

A crackling leaf amidst the distant tree-line – barely audible, but crystal clear to Mary's ears – startled her. She brought the redwood stock of the carbine up to her shoulder and scanned the tree-line as she gazed through the weapon's iron sights.

Scores of glowing, crimson dots appeared among the trees, each floating – in pairs – two or three feet off the ground.

"Damn," Mary gasped. "Night Howlers!"

She pulled the carbine's trigger. A silver bullet exploded from the weapon's muzzle and sped toward the floating red dots.

A moment later, a pair of dots faded as a yelp of agony echoed across the night sky.

Mary leapt to her feet and sprinted toward her horseless carriage, which sat a few yards away.

A tremendous growl rose from the tree-line as the Night Howlers charged out of the forest.

Mary peered over her shoulder at the beasts closing on her. There were easily five dozen of them – the largest pack she had ever seen. The creatures were a monstrous mix of man and wolf. Some had the body of a large wolf, but the head of a man or woman; others walked upright, like men, but still possessed lupine fur and features; while still others had the bodies of men and the countenances of wolves.

Mary hopped into the driver's seat of the horseless carriage and furiously pumped the brass handle, which protruded from the floor of the cart, until a cloud of steam rose from a bronze stack at the rear of the carriage. She then squeezed the trigger on the brass handle and the vehicle lurched forward.

The horseless carriage – powered by highly compressed steam – picked up speed and was soon cruising along at a good pace.

The Night Howlers, however, were faster.

A wolf-creature, with the ruddy, angular face of a young – and rabid – woman, sprang onto the back of the carriage.

The smell of musk and fresh dirt assaulted Mary's nostrils.

The massive creature swiped with its right forepaw, slashing at Mary's back with its razor-sharp claws.

Mary's dress shredded and a deep red welt formed across her sinewy back.

A perplexed expression spread across the wolf creature's rubicund face.

Black Mary turned in her chair, reached back and grabbed the monster by its throat. "Wondering why I ain't open up like a turkey shop on Thanksgiving, huh?" Mary chuckled. "'Skin like stone', the docs say. Now, let's see what your skin is like."

The big woman drove the tips of her fingers into the Night Howler's neck.

A hissing sound escaped the creature's mouth as Black Mary forcefully yanked her hand backward, ripping out the Howler's windpipe.

The Howler fell from the carriage and landed – in a heap – on the grass.

Another Night Howler – this one of the upright wolf variety – rushed toward the steam-powered carriage.

Mary aimed her carbine and fired.

The Night Howler collapsed as the silver bullet speared through its chest and burst from its back.

Suddenly, the steam-carriage stopped.

Black Mary looked back over her shoulder. Two Night Howlers were crouched at the back of the carriage; their claws dug into the oaken frame of the vehicle. The creatures' muscles strained – veins rising from beneath fur and flesh – as they held the carriage in place.

Mary dropped the carbine and drew two Colt Dragoon revolvers from under her seat. She fired both weapons. A round struck each Night Howler between its eyebrows.

The pair of Howlers fell, but their purpose had been well-served, for Mary suddenly found herself in the midst of a deluge of rabid monsters.

The cart could not move.

Mary fired round after searing round into the slobbering mob of Night Howlers as they clawed and bit her flesh.

Although Black Mary's flesh was as impenetrable as granite, the manifold superficial wounds she suffered weakened her and she began to feel light-headed.

Suddenly, what appeared to be a snake fell in front of Black Mary's face.

The big woman jerked her head back and saw that what fell was not a snake at all, but was, in fact, a rope.

Mary followed the rope, with her gaze, up to its source – *the Nefertiti*, which hovered above her.

Mary wrapped the rope in her fist and yanked on it.

The Nefertiti rose, pulling Black Mary upward and away from the clutches of the Night Howlers, who snarled and wailed madly in the darkness.

The airship sped away, pulling Black Mary in tow.

The woman breathed a sigh of relief and then smiled, enjoying the cool night air as it caressed her face.

CHAPTER 47

May 5, 1865

Harriet pounded on the polished brass double doors. Above her, a sign that read 'Palais de Madame D'Oliva' shook from the force.

The doors slowly opened – by some invisible power – revealing a grand foyer, constructed of mahogany. A plush, oxblood carpet covered the floor. At the center of the capacious foyer sat a mahogany, spiral staircase, covered in the same oxblood carpeting as the floor.

The smell of Egyptian Musk incense greeted Harriet as she stepped into the brothel.

"*Mamzelle Harriet*," a rich bass voice crooned.

Harriet snapped her head to her right, toward the sound of the voice. Standing before her, tipping his oxblood derby with his head bowed, stood a tall, athletically built man of middle-age. The man's dark skin was in sharp contrast to the white, full dress tail coat of his tuxedo.

"Marcel," Harriet replied with a smile. "How are you?"

"Better than ever," Marcel answered. "And how are you?"

"I've seen better days; but the Lawd still allowin' me to draw breath, so I ain't complainin'," Harriet replied.

"And how may the Palais de Madame D'Oliva be of service?" Marcel inquired.

"I am here to beg a favor of Madame D'Oliva," Harriet answered. "I need a horse and some guns…maybe a little food."

"I am afraid Madame D'Oliva is not here," Marcel said. "She will be in the company of Professor Kleinhopper for the next few days, but you are welcome to take one of the rooms until Madame returns."

“I can’t wait that long,” Harriet replied. “Any way you can get a message to Madame D’Oliva or direct me to this Professor…”

“Kleinhopper,” Marcel said. “He is the owner of the ‘Karnival of Konstructs’”.

A chill embraced Harriet. “Constructs?”

“Yes, mechanical creatures, given life through the power of alchemy,” Marcel said.

“The Alchemist,” Harriet whispered.

“Pardon?”

“I’ll be needin' that room after all.”

CHAPTER 48

May 6, 1865

Black Mary rummaged under a seat at the rear of *The Nefertiti*, tossing aside a suede water-skin and a small oak chessboard. "Got anymore jerky, Baas? I'm so hungry, my stomach is startin' to think my throat is cut."

Baas shook his head. "You ate all of the jerky – ten pounds of it, I might add – about three hours ago."

"How do you expect me to do some killin' on an empty stomach?" Mary asked, pouting.

"We will stop for supplies and to refuel in about an hour," Baas replied. "I promise – I will buy you whatever you want to eat then."

"An hour?" Black Mary sighed. "Okay, but I'm warnin' you, Baas, I don't eat like a bird like your tiny, little girlfriend, Harriet."

"I gathered that," Baas sighed.

"Speakin' of Miss Holy Roller, why didn't you get *her* to help you? She *loves* killin'."

"Harriet doesn't love killing," Baas said. "She does what she must to fulfill her mission."

Mary rolled her eyes. "Harriet Tubman loves killin' more than a fat man loves cake."

"In answer to your question," Baas snapped. "Harriet ventured into Mexico to resolve an issue and has yet to return.

"I'm sure her precious 'Lawd' will see her through," Mary snickered.

"A bit of faith might do you some good, Mary Fields,"

"I got faith," Mary said, drawing her twin revolvers from the holsters strapped to her waist. "Faith in my fists and in my skills with these Colt Dragoons."

“Ah, the Church of Violence,” Baas said.

“Amen, brother,” Mary replied, holstering her weapons. “Amen!”

CHAPTER 49

May 8, 1865

"*That will be fifty cents, Monsieur*."

Harriet handed the young man working the box office a shiny silver coin. The young man pulled a lever in the booth and the waist-high gate before Harriet swung open.

"Go right in, Monsieur," the young man said.

"Thank you," Harriet replied as she walked past the '*White's Only*' sign and stepped through the gateway.

She looked skyward and whispered – "And thank *you*, Lawd, for once again confoundin' the senses of my enemies."

Harriet followed the excited throng toward a massive, circular tent. The tent's conical roof was lined with white lights that blinked off and on in a steady rhythm.

"Aether-powered torchlight," Harriet whispered. "The Lawd done definitely guided me right."

Harriet entered the tent. More 'aether lights' lined it, providing just enough illumination for the carnival-goers to avoid bumping into someone as they took their seats.

Harriet sat five rows from the stage, around which sat a group of mechanical men, powered by the clockwork that hummed and ticked in their chests. Each mechanical man possessed a musical instrument for a head – a pair of trumpet-headed men; a trombone; a tuba; a trio of fifes; a bass drum; and a pair of snares.

The robot band broke into a lively tune – '*When Johnny Comes Marching Home*', which the playbill claimed was written by the band's human composer, Patrick Gilmore – as patrons poured into the tent.

The lights faded and gave way to darkness as *When Johnny Comes Marching Home* reached its crescendo.

The band's music finally surrendered to silence and for a few moments the crowded tent was completely still and blanketed in blackness.

And then, a voice rent the quiescence – "*Aristocrats…patricians…ladies, gentlemen, uppercrusters and thoroughbreds…*"

A spotlight above the stage came to life with a loud pop.

Gasps rose from the audience as the source of the voice was revealed. Standing before them, center-stage, was a tall, lean man, dressed in the livery of a Plague Doctor – a black leather mask with polished, silver-framed goggle lenses for eyes and a shiny, silver beak, reminiscent of a toucan; a black, form-fitting jumpsuit that stretched from just below his chin, down into his black leather boots; black leather gloves, which fit like a second skin; a black leather frock; and a top-hat, also crafted of black leather.

"For centuries, man has delighted in the spectacle called 'the carnival'," the man said, raising the black walking cane he clutched in his right hand above his head. "Or, in Latin, *the carne vale – farewell to the flesh.*"

The stage lights reflected off of the silver tip of the man's cane, which was cast in the image of a grinning skull.

"Tonight," the man continued. "We say 'farewell to the flesh' as we hail the rise of the mechanical and the magical coming together as one!"

The man leapt high into the air, twisting and somersaulting gracefully before landing upon one knee, with his head bowed low. "Ladies and gentlemen, I am Professor Amschel Kleinhopper – alchemist extraordinaire…"

Professor Kleinhopper sprang to his feet and flung his arms out widely. "And I welcome you all…to Kleinhopper's Karnival of Konstructs!"

Suddenly, a cloud of black smoke – accompanied by a thunderous boom – engulfed Professor Kleinhopper. When the smoke cleared a moment later, the Professor was gone and standing on the stage were three knolls – one, the size of the creatures Harriet fought…the creatures that killed Baas Bello's beloved son-in-law, Talltrees – the other two, the size of toddlers, but just as monstrous.

More gasps – and even a few frightened cries – rose from the audience.

The pair of small knolls climbed the giant one, using their gargantuan brother like a jungle-gym – leaping and swinging from one of the giant's outstretched arms to the other; climbing to the top of its head and diving into one of the colossus' palms; and other feats of derring-do.

The audience's fear of the creatures gave way to awe and soon, the tent erupted into raucous applause.

"He makes evil fair-seeming, Lawd," Harriet whispered.

As the night of spectacle went on, Professor Kleinhopper's knolls continued to amaze – as did the Professor himself, with his skillful displays of acrobatics and prestidigitation.

By the show's end, everyone in the audience was on his or her feet, clapping and whistling in approval of a presentation unlike anything they had ever experienced.

Harriet squeezed through the adoring crowd and exited the tent. She perused the queue of carts, carriages and covered wagons parked behind the tent. Each had *Kleinhopper's Karnival of Konstructs* embossed, in brass lettering, on their sides.

Under the cover of shadows, Harriet crept toward the vehicles and then slithered under a cart. "Walk with me, Lawd," she whispered; and then, taking hold of the undercarriage, she pulled herself up and out of sight.

CHAPTER 50

May 8, 1865

The procession of vehicles came to a halt.

The smell of freshwater and the sound of gently breaking waves told Harriet that she was at the Mississippi River.

"Get the vehicles on board and feed the horses," she heard Kleinhopper say. "Then, rest well, my children; we head upriver in the morning…oh, and dump Madame D'Oliva's remains in the river, please. Goodnight."

Harriet felt a slight bump, followed by the intermittent sound of wood pelting metal as the wagon, under which she hid, traversed the steel bridge.

A few moments later, the pelting sound gave way to the sound of the heavy, wooden wheels of the cart rolling across a wooden floor.

The cart shook as man-sized and toddler-sized knolls exited the vehicle. Massive legs shambled past Harriet, shaking the deck with each step.

A few minutes later, all was quiet. Harriet lowered herself to the floor. She lay there for a moment, stretching her aching back and stiffened fingers, and then rolled from under the cart.

Harriet scanned the area. All was still.

Crouching low, she crept toward a spiral staircase that rose before her.

Harriet paused, taking a moment to study her surroundings. She was on a riverboat of incredible craftsmanship. The floor and walls were constructed from ebony. Etched into the hard, dark wood were symbols similar to those tattooed upon the face of an old Chinese assassin she once encountered. Harriet wondered if Professor Kleinhopper would be as difficult to kill as that assassin.

Harriet crawled up the stairs, her light steps further muffled by the plush Persian carpentry that ran up the center of each step.

At the top of the stairway, Harriet quietly dropped to her belly and perused her surroundings. The floor was covered in the same rich carpeting as the spiral staircase. The ebon walls were covered with paintings of – and, most likely, from – exotic Eastern lands, of which Harriet had dreamed of visiting since she first heard tales of such places from Baas Bello. Baas had visited nearly every country in the world. Harriet recognized – from Baas' vivid descriptions – an armor-clad Japanese samurai striking a red-faced demon with his gleaming katana; a Maori queen, riding upon the back of a giant blue whale; a pair of boxers from Thailand, fighting from the back of an elephant…

"*An art aficionado, eh?*"

Harriet whirled around toward the voice.

No one stood before her.

She snapped her head upward.

Clinging to the high ceiling, like a spider, was Professor Amschel Kleinhopper. "Unfortunately, you will soon be dead, so you purchasing a piece is not an option."

The Professor dropped from the ceiling. His billowing frock and Plague Doctor's mask gave him the appearance of a bird of smoke and shadow.

Harriet leapt upward, grabbing Professor Kleinhopper's neck in mid-air.

Upon their descent, Harriet snapped the Professor's head toward the floor with a powerful jerk.

Just before The Professor's skull met the hardwood floor, however, he vanished in a puff of black smoke.

A swishing sound came from behind Harriet. She rolled forward, barely evading the pulverizing strike from Professor Kleinhopper's cane.

Harriet peered over her shoulder. Professor Kleinhopper knelt on one knee. A spider web-shaped crack in the floor extended from the tip of his cane.

"You have chosen to purloin from the wrong gentleman, Miss…"

"Tubman," Harriet replied. "Harriet Tubman; and I ain't come to steal; I came to settle a score for a dear friend."

"Wait…you are the woman who accompanied Baas Bello," Professor Kleinhopper said.

"That's right," Harriet replied.

"You are quite…talented," Professor Kleinhopper said. "I have no quarrel with you. Baas Bello – and that fool son-in-law of his – were my intended targets."

"Why? Why Talltrees? Why Baas?" Harriet asked.

"*Because he is an envious child.*"

"Baas Bello!" Professor Kleinhopper hissed, turning to face the old genius.

"Are you okay, Harriet?" Baas asked, pointing his Bello Rifle at Professor Kleinhopper's throat.

"I'm fine, Baas," Harriet replied. "I was just about to kill The Alchemist, is all. How *you* be?"

"No, Harriet, this one is mine," Baas replied.

Two shots rang out from below them, followed by a ghastly scream.

"But, please," Baas continued. "Mary can use your assistance downstairs. It would appear the knolls have awakened."

"Mary?" Harriet said, shaking her head. "Black Mary Fields?"

"That would be her," Baas replied. "Now, please, if you will…"

Harriet darted past Baas and scurried down the stairs.

Black Mary was busy dodging blows from the twin toddler-sized knolls, a pair of man-sized knoll and a giant knoll as she fired her twin revolvers.

A hammering backhand to her chest from the gargantuan knoll sent Mary sliding backward.

As she slid past Harriet, she nodded and smiled. "Evenin', Harriet."

"Hello, Mary," Harriet replied dryly.

Mary's back slammed into the wall behind her. She bounced off the wall and leapt forward, slamming her elbow into the clockwork that was the heart of a charging knoll. Gears, chain links and a haze of steam flew into the air. The knoll fell.

A squad of toddler-sized knolls charged toward Harriet.

"Catch," Mary shouted, tossing one of her Colt Dragoons to her.

Harriet plucked the pistol out of the air and – with blinding speed – fanned the revolver's hammer as she repeatedly squeezed the trigger.

Knoll after tiny knoll fell, screaming in agony as oil, dirt, gears and stone peppered the walls and floor.

Suddenly, a massive hand of grass and soil grabbed Mary and plucked her from the floor, hoisting her high into the air.

A loud, cracking noise came from within the gargantuan knoll's fist.

"Mary!" Harriet screamed, fearing that the cracking noise was the sound of Black Mary's bones being crushed to dust.

Oil dripped from the creature's fist and it unleashed a wail that shook the entire riverboat. The giant knoll's injured hand sprang open, revealing a smoking hole made by Black Mary's Colt Dragoon.

Mary wrapped her muscular arms around the giant's thumb and then forcefully arched backward as she raised her arms high above her head.

The giant knoll released what could only be described as a gasp of shock as it was turned upside down, its feet leaving a trail of dirt and grass across the ceiling as it careened through the air.

The creature landed on its back with a tremendous thud. A torrent of steam erupted from its mouth.

"Lawd," Harriet whispered, impressed by Black Mary's tremendous strength.

Mary landed on her feet next to the giant corpse's head. She raised her fists to her chin. "Come on, y'all; I'm just warmin' up!"

****

"Have you told your daughter that her husband is dead, Baas?" Professor Kleinhopper snickered, as he crept toward Baas' right.

The old genius followed the Professor's movements with the muzzle of his rifle. "I'll tell her as I'm handing her your head in a box," Baas replied.

"Do you think death frightens me, old man?" Professor Kleinhopper spat. "I welcome it. Thanks to you though, that is a gift forever denied me."

"You were playing God, Benjamin," Baas sighed. "Reanimating corpses…using *my* technology to create new life…"

"You tricked me into donning this accursed mask!" Professor Kleinhopper hissed, slapping the Plague Doctor mask with the palm of his hand.

"*You* wanted to be like me…immortal; *you* stole the Athanasia Masquerade; *you* put it on; you got what you wanted," Baas said with a shrug.

"When did you realize that The Alchemist is me?"

"When I saw your show. The mask…the way you move; it has been sixty years, but there is much about you that I recall, Benjamin." Baas replied.

"Benjamin Banneker is dead, old man," Professor Kleinhopper growled. "I am now – and forever more – Professor Amschel Kleinhopper!"

Baas fired the Bello rifle.

Professor Kleinhopper staggered backward a few steps before collapsing onto his back.

Baas slowly approached the unmoving Professor until he stood over the man's masked face. "The bullet has severed the connection between your cerebellum and your spine. You are permanently - irreparably – paralyzed. You *will* live forever Benjamin…as a quadriplegic."

Baas turned on his heels and slowly walked away.

"No!" Professor Kleinhopper screamed. "I'm going to kill you, Baas Bello…I'm going to kill your daughter…I am going to destroy all that you hold dear! Do you hear me, old man? *Do you hear me*?!"

****

Harriet spotted a fast movement in her peripheral vision. She looked up from the man-sized knoll she held under her boot heel and spotted Baas Bello sprinting down the stairs. She thrust the jagged stone thigh bone of a freshly killed giant knoll into the clockwork in the man-sized knoll's chest. The knoll shuddered and then went limp.

Harriet examined the carnage on the lower deck. Dead knolls lay everywhere. The floor was covered in slick, brown oil and pieces of copper. The air reeked of petroleum, bronze and wet grass.

Mary leaned against the wall nearest to the staircase, drinking a bottle of cognac. "It ain't whiskey, but it's still pretty good. That Professor Kleinhopper had good taste."

"*Has* good taste," Baas replied, correcting her.

"*Has*?" Harriet asked, stepping away from the dead knolls and toward Baas. "The Alchemist ain't dead?"

"Well, I can change that," Mary bellowed as she dashed toward the stairs. "Be back in a second."

"Leave him," Baas said. "He is in Hell; Talltrees is vindicated."

"Cryptic li'l fella, ain't ya?" Mary said, shaking her head.

"Well, if we're done her, I need your help, Baas," Harriet said.

"What is going on, Harriet?" Baas asked.

"John Brown ain't dead," Harriet replied. "He a spirit; got the power to possess bodies. He possessed John Wilkes Booth…and my nephew, Ben. He set me up for murder and kidnappin' and now he plans to possess Frederick Douglass."

"What?" Baas gasped. "And why Frederick?"

"He gon' use him to start a war, in my name, between negroes and white folks." Harriet replied.

"Let us make haste off this steamboat and get to *The Nefertiti*," Baas said. "Please, give me a full account on the way."

"Hey, count me in," Black Mary said, tossing the now empty bottle of cognac over her shoulder. "Freddy Douglass looks tastier than a plate of plum pudding!

Harriet rolled her eyes. Baas Bello nudged her gently with his elbow.

"Glad to have you, Mary," Harriet sighed.

CHAPTER 51

May 9, 1865

Rochester, New York was uncharacteristically chilly and the wind was strong and crisp.

Frederick Douglass sat at his desk, drinking a cup of hot peppermint tea and staring out the window at the clear, morning sky.

A short, stout figure appeared in the doorway of Douglass' office.

"Come in, sir," Frederick Douglass said.

The man stepped into the office and tipped his John Bull top-hat. "Bonjour, Monsieur Douglass, I am Louis Pasteur."

"Welcome, Dr. Pasteur," Douglass said, pointing toward a cherry oak chair. "Please, take a seat."

John Brown sat down and flashed a broad smile. He ran his thick fingers across his full, white beard as he placed his top-hat in his lap. "I must say, Monsieur Douglass, I – and my colleagues admire your work tremendously and we look forward to your lecture tour of France."

"I thank you for your sponsorship, Dr. Pasteur," Frederick Douglass said.

"Would you be ready to leave next month?" John Brown asked. "If you leave then, we should be able to commence in mid-August. The tour will conclude in early October and we should have you home in time for the Winter Solstice."

"June would be perfect," Douglass replied.

"Then I will have your ticket and your itinerary to you within the week," John Brown said, extending his hand.

Frederick Douglass took Louis Pasteur's / John Brown's hand in his and shook it briskly. Suddenly, John Brown yanked Frederick Douglass' arm, pulling him across the table.

"What…what are you doing?" Douglass shouted.

"Taking your place," John Brown whispered.

John Brown then opened his mouth wide and bit down into Frederick Douglass' neck.

Suddenly, John Brown staggered backward, his hands pressed to his face. A trickle of blood slithered down his chin.

Frederick Douglass smiled as he picked up the pieces of Pasteur's broken teeth from his desk. "Hurts, don't it?"

"How? How did you…?" John Brown stuttered.

The illusion faded.

Standing before John Brown was a grinning Mary Fields.

"I didn't," Mary replied. "*She* did."

John Brown looked over his shoulder. Harriet's fist slammed into his jaw.

John Brown collapsed, falling on his face at Harriet's feet.

"Now, step aside and let me stomp this boy's head into wine," Mary said.

"No," Harriet said. "I need him to tell me where my nephew, Ben, is first."

"I know a voodoo queen back west that can throw some shells and tell you where your nephew is at," Black Mary said. "We need to kill this monster, now!"

"I said, not yet!" Harriet shouted.

"You don't run this show," Mary said, stepping toward Harriet. "You'd best watch your tone!"

Baas Bello peeked into the room. "You two can kill each other – and John Brown – later; however, at the present moment, we need to get this monster to *The Nefertiti* before he wakes up."

Black Mary snatched up John Brown the seat of his pants and carried him, like a satchel, out of the office.

"You need to find a way to keep the peace with Black Mary," Baas whispered. "The only one among us Gifted with more physical strength is Mama Maybelle; she possesses the audial senses equivalent to a cat; the olfactory senses of a bloodhound; and she is nigh indestructible. *Not* someone you want as an enemy."

"True," Harriet replied. "I'm sure the Lawd will show me the way."

"I am sure He will," Baas said. "Now, let's get to the airship before Mary decides to go ahead and kill John Brown."

CHAPTER 52

May 9, 1865

Ben and Rit sat on Harriet's porch, relaxing in their twin rocking chairs, enjoying the brisk morning air.

The rest of the neighborhood was quiet.

"No sign of Harriet yet," a gaunt-faced man whispered, lowering a spyglass from his eye.

"I was sure that home would be the next place Harriet would run to," Caleb said, stepping out of the shadows cast by the trees. "Take four of our best men to check out the house."

The gaunt-faced ghul nodded and then perused the regiment of his brethren. He picked his squad quickly and then the detachment took off toward Harriet's house like greyhounds exploding out of their traps at the start of a race.

Ben and Rit spotted the charging monstrosities. The couple rose as quickly from their rocking chairs as their aged bodies would allow, but the ghuls were just too fast and pounced upon the elderly couple, driving them into the house as if they were stray cattle.

"We'll be snacking on dark meat today, boys!" Caleb shouted.

A fearsome cheer rose from the monstrous horde.

A moment later, Ben and Rit returned to the porch and resumed rocking in their chairs.

"What the hell?" Caleb exclaimed, a dribble of yellow-green saliva escaping the torn corner of his mouth. "It's gotta be Harriet! She *is* in there!"

Caleb pointed toward Harriet's front porch. "Everybody, take the house, but do not kill Harriet! Bring her to *me*!"

The Ghul Army charged toward the house, beating small craters into the soft grass beneath their heels.

The Ghul Army came to a shuddering halt as a sea of dark blue flooded out of every nearby house as hundreds of Union soldiers sprang out of hiding.

"It's a trap," Caleb shouted, looking back over his shoulder at the creatures in his charge. "Skedaddle! Harriet has sprang a trap!"

"*Not Harriet, monster.*"

Caleb looked toward Harriet's porch. Standing before him was Edwin Stanton calmly smoking a cigar. Mama Maybelle stood beside him. The giantess' hands rested firmly on her hips.

"Stanton! Blood don't have to spill here today," Caleb said. "Just give up Harriet Tubman and me and my boys will be on our way."

"Harriet is dead," Stanton replied. "And blood *does* have to spill."

"If Harriet's dead, why are you here?"

"Have you forgotten what you did to my daughter?!"

"Yep," Caleb replied. "I remade her…in *my* image and likeness."

"You're no god," Stanton replied.

"Ye are all gods; children of the most high God," Caleb shot back. "Now, ain't that what Jesus said to his disciples? They was Gifted…like Jesus; like *us*."

"And, like Jesus, you are about to be crucified," Stanton said, snapping his fingers. "But you *won't* be rising from *your* grave."

A loud rumble echoed across the sky. From behind Harriet's house, marched into view a man of metal that stood nearly two stories tall and three times as wide as a man. In lieu of hands, the towering man possessed a pair of six-barreled Gatling guns; protruding from each iron shoulder was a chimney that belched cones of white steam.

The metal man's face was constructed of thick, transpicuous amber and a flesh-and-blood man was visible inside the construct's head.

Caleb recognized the man from the saloon in Texas, where Mama Maybelle and Druga massacred the fool patrons. The man had come to clean up. He was Edwin Stanton's right-hand man, Caleb recalled. "Colonel Conger!"

Colonel Conger sat inside the giant's head, his hands clutching a pair of levers. The Colonel pressed a pedal with his left foot and the mechanical man assumed a low, wide fighting stance.

The corners of Stanton's lips curled upward into a smile.

Caleb roared madly and then charged toward Harriet's front porch.

Colonel Conger rapidly squeezed and released the spring-loaded handles on the levers. Fire erupted from the man-tank's Gatling gun-hands as round after round exploded from the guns' muzzles in rapid succession.

Scores of ghuls were ripped to shreds under the brutal volley of bullets.

The Union soldiers unleashed a hail of hot iron from their Henry rifles and many more ghuls fell.

Caleb leapt onto the porch and thrust forward with his fingers, which were now fused together into twin spears.

Stanton side-stepped Caleb's thrusts as he drew his Colt Dragoon from the holster on his hip.

The Secretary of War fired under Caleb's outstretched arm, firing a round into the monster's ribcage.

Caleb's torso-face gasped in agony and he fell to one knee, coughing blood from the torn "mouth" in his lower torso.

Stanton pulled back the hammer of the revolver and pressed the weapon to Caleb's upper chest – right at the center of his "forehead".

As Stanton squeezed the trigger, he felt a sharp, biting pain in his inner, right thigh. Caleb's limp body rolled down the steps and landed, in a bloody heap, at the feet of the mechanical man.

Colonel Conger pressed a pedal with his right heel. The mechanical man's right knee sprang up to the height of its waist and then shot downward, driving the heel of its massive iron foot toward Caleb.

The General of the Ghul Army disappeared under the mechanical giant's foot. A moment later, greenish-black ichor sprayed from beneath the iron colossus' heel.

Stanton collapsed against Mama Maybelle.

"You alright, child?" Maybelle asked, laying Stanton gently onto his back on the porch.

"No, Mama," Stanton replied, pointing toward his trousers, which were now soaked with blood. "He got me good."

"Hold on, son," Maybelle cried. I'll get you to a medic," Maybelle cried. Tears ran, in rivers, down her plump cheeks.

"Too late for that, Mama," Stanton said weakly. "My femoral artery is severed; I am beyond help. Please, just…just stay with me, Mama."

Mama Maybelle cradled Stanton's head in her arms. "A mama ain't supposed to watch her child die; it ain't right!"

Stanton smiled. "You're an immortal; this is not the first time and it won't be the last."

"Don't make it no easier, child," Mama Maybelle sighed.

"Keep Margaret safe," Stanton said. "We cured her body but her mind…"

"I will, child," Mama Maybelle replied. "I know a woman who'll have her right as rain in no time."

"Good," Stanton said, closing his eyes. "I love you, Mama. Tell Margaret…"

"I will, child," Maybelle whispered, gingerly laying Stanton's head on the porch.

The giantess stood and perused the carnage in Harriet's front yard. A handful of ghuls were still alive and they were running for their lives with squads of Union soldiers – and Colonel Conger's mechanical man – in hot pursuit.

Mama Maybelle turned toward Ben and Rit. "I'm sorry for your loss. Harriet was a good woman and a great warrior."

"Just leave us be," Ben said.

"Fair enough," Maybelle replied, picking up her son and tossing his corpse over her shoulder. The giantess then bent her knees deeply and then exploded upward. With two powerful leaps, she disappeared from sight.

"Our baby is gone, Ben!" Rit cried, burying her face in the palms of her hands.

"Hush up, Rit," Ben replied. "Harriet ain't no mo' dead than you and me is white!"

"What you mean, Ben?"

"Search yo' soul," Ben answered. "Do you feel any loss?"

"Naw," Rit said, pressing her hands to the belly that once carried her beloved Harriet. "Naw, I don't."

"A daddy *know*," Ben said. "And a mama shol' '*nuff* know! Until I see fo' myself, I ain't believin' it."

"We did raise a tough one in Harriet, didn't we?" Rit said.

"Tougher than the Devil's toenails," Ben replied. "Tougher than the Devil's toenails!"

CHAPTER 53

May 9, 1865

John Brown laughed as his nose shattered under the force of Harriet's punch. "Nice one, General Tubman! I'm still not telling you, but that was a nice punch all the same."

"Tell me where Ben is, or as the Lawd is my witness, I'll break every bone in your body," Harriet spat.

"Do it, General Tubman," John Brown snickered. "Destroy Pasteur's body; I'll find another, eventually, and the game will begin anew."

"No, it will not," Baas said, sauntering to the rear of *The Nefertiti*. He opened his left hand, revealing a box of matches. He plucked one match from the box and struck it on John Brown's forehead. "Throughout Africa, the people fear being burned."

Baas waved the lit match in front of John Brown's face. The flame danced an inch from John Brown's nose. "We fear being burned because we know that fire is the only thing on earth that can permanently destroy a spirit.

Baas blew out the flame and tossed the smoldering match into John Brown's lap. "Burn a man's body while he still lives and the spirit dies with him. Heaven is forever lost to him."

Baas lit another match. John Brown recoiled away from it.

"Aah, you understand," Baas said, smiling. "You will tell Harriet where Ben is *now*, or I promise you – after Harriet is done with you – I will reduce you to ash."

"Alright…alright," John Brown cried. "The boy is in the care of a dear, old friend of yours, Baas…I believe you know her too, Harriet…"

"Her?" Harriet inquired.

"Yes," John Brown snickered. "You're going to have to head back to New Orleans and pay a visit to the woman Harriet stole your heart from, Baas Bello."

"What? No!" Baas gasped.

"Oh, yes," John Brown chuckled. "I left Ben in the care of the most powerful sorcerer on the continent, Baas Bello!"

Baas shook his head. "No!"

"Who?" Black Mary asked.

"Marie Laveau," Harriet croaked.

"Your ex-wife, isn't she, Baas?" John Brown snickered.

Harriet felt ill. Marie Laveau hated her. After all, *she* was the object of affection of Madame Laveau's beloved Baas Bello.

"Baas, you old rake," Mary giggled. "Count me in again; I wouldn't miss *this* one!"

"By the way, she is still furious that you took her daughter from her when you left," John Brown said.

"Shut your mouth!" Baas shouted. "Bela *chose* to go with me. Her mother had grown corrupt…proven by the fact she now associates with the likes of you!"

"You're all going to die! John Brown snickered.

Black Mary pounced on John Brown, clutching his head between her massive hands. With a powerful pull, she twisted his head until his chin rested squarely between his shoulder blades. "Damn, you talk too much!"

John Brown collapsed in his chair.

"Mary," Harriet gasped. "What have you done?"

"What you wouldn't," Mary replied.

"If he was lying about Ben's whereabouts, we'll never find my nephew," Harriet spat.

"Oh, please," Mary said, rolling her eyes. "He weren't lyin' and you *know* it. What were you gon' do, Harriet? Wait for the *Lawd* to tell you when to torture and kill the man?"

"The Lawd always guide me right," Harriet replied.

"Then, ask him where you should dump this fool's body; I'm about to get me some shut-eye."

"We'll cremate him when we land on the outskirts of New Orleans," Baas said, pulling a brass lever on *The Nefertiti's* control panel.

The airship jerked forward as the rotor at the airship's rear began to turn.

"Harriet, can you give her some steam, please?" Baas asked.

Harriet stood at the rear of the airship and grasped the throttle. She pushed the lever upward and then snatched it downward.

A cloud of steam rose from the airship's stack and then *The Nefertiti* rose.

"Lawd, though I walk in the midst of trouble," Harriet whispered, turning her face skyward. "Please, protect me from death's cold embrace. Stretch out your hands against my enemies, Lawd and deliver me to victory."

"While you at it, ask him to deliver me one of them alligator hoagies when we get to the French Quarter," Mary said.

Harriet shook her head.

"Where to now?" Black Mary asked.

"We're sixty-four miles outside of Auburn, New York – Harriet's home town," Baas replied. "That's less than an hour away. I figure Harriet can spend a couple of hours with her parents and then we can refuel and be on our way to New Orleans."

"Well, let's burn him when we get there," Mary said, nodding toward Louis Pasteur's corpse. "If not, he'll be pretty rank by the time we get to N'arlins."

"I concur," Baas said. "Harriet?"

"Alright," Harriet replied. "I have a fire-pit at the back of my house; you can do it there while I talk to my folks."

"A fire-pit?" Mary inquired, rubbing her palms together gleefully. "Let's buy a few slabs of beef ribs and have ourselves a barbecue!"

"A barbecue? Right after incinerating a man on that very same pit?" Baas asked, shaking his head.

"Why let a good fire go to waste?" Black Mary replied.

"Have you ever read Shakespeare, Mary?" Baas asked. "He had a flare for the macabre…like you; I think you'd enjoy reading his work."

"I don't read no more, Baas," Mary replied.

"You don't read anymore? Why not?" Baas inquired.

"Well, I read that smokin' peyote was bad, so I stopped smokin' peyote; I read that eatin' pork was bad, so I stopped eatin' pork; I read that drinkin' whiskey was bad…so I stopped *readin'*."

Baas burst into laughter.

Harriet tried not to, but found herself laughing at Mary's joke, too.

"What? She laughs?" Mary chuckled, pointing at Harriet.

"The Lawd says 'a joyful heart is good medicine'," Harriet replied.

"Then loosen up, sit with me a spell and call me 'Doctor Fields'," Mary said.

"After we take Ben off of Marie Laveau's hands, I'll take you up on that," Harriet said.

Harriet peered out of a porthole at the rear of the airship. The sky had grown black as pitch. "And I beheld when he opened the sixth seal…the sun became as black as sackcloth of hair and the moon became as blood…for the great day of His wrath is come; and who shall be able to stand?"

CHAPTER 54

May 9, 1865

The giantess sat in the elegant parlor, tapping a staccato rhythm with her sizable feet. Maybelle's plump fingers were wrapped around Margaret's tiny wrist.

Margaret rocked back and forth, wincing as she let loose a symphony of frightful grunts and moans.

"I am so hungry, Mama Maybelle," Margaret whined. "So hungry."

"We just ate, child," Mama Maybelle replied. "Breathe…calm yourself like I showed you."

"I am trying to calm myself, but I cannot," Margaret cried. Tears fell down her cheeks, which were – once again – plump and rosy. "The lunch we just had was burned. I want something else to eat."

"That steak was cooked rare, child," Mama Maybelle sighed. "It wasn't burned at all. The sickness has you craving raw flesh, child."

"You're going to help me get better, right?" Margaret asked.

"I *am, cher.*"

Margaret looked up into the kind eyes of a venerable woman dressed – from head to toe – in pristine white.

The woman's curly, white hair – as pristine as her blouse, skirt and fuzzy slippers – peeked out from under her intricately tied head-wrap.

She extended her café au lait-toned hand toward Margaret. "I am Madame Marie Laveau, cher; I am a good friend of your grandmother, here."

Mama Maybelle lowered her gaze.

"My grandmother?" Margaret giggled. "You have the wrong Margaret, ma'am."

Marie Laveau placed a hand on Mama Maybelle's shoulder. "Ah, she don't know."

"She does now, child," Mama Maybelle sighed.

"I…I do not understand," Margaret said. "How can you be my grandmother, Mama Maybelle? You are a…a *negro*!"

"Pere Legba got a message for you, baby," Marie Laveau said. "He say, *you* a negro too, so watch your tone, cher."

Tears welled in the corners of Margaret's eyes. "But, how?"

"Edwin…your father…he's my son, child," Mama Maybelle replied. "That's how he got The Gift; how *you* got it too."

"Me?" Margaret replied. "I am nobody special. Daddy does say that I am his princess, though."

"You *are* one of the Gifted, child," Mama Maybelle said. "That's why you still have the ghul hunger, even though your flesh has been cured. Your *soul* is holding on to the infection."

"Pere Legba say, yo' soul strong," Marie Laveau chimed in. "Stronger than most; which is why I gotta go in and whoop yo' soul into submission, cher."

"Whoop my soul?" Margaret inquired.

"You ever heard the sayin' 'I'm gon' beat the devil outta you'?" Marie Laveau asked.

"Yes, ma'am," Margaret replied.

"Well, cher, that's *just* what I'm gon' do!"

"Is my daddy going to be here soon?" Margaret asked, a tear rolling down her cheek. "I want my daddy! This is just too much!"

Marie placed her palm upon Margaret's forehead. "Calm yourself, cher."

Margaret's eyes rolled back in her head and then the girl collapsed, her head coming to rest on one of Mama Maybelle's plump thighs.

"Be right back, Mere Maybelle," Madame Laveau said, exiting the parlor with grace and verve.

Few minutes later, the old voodoo queen returned, carrying a large, black hen. The bird's wings were held firmly in her right hand and its feet clutched tightly in her left.

"Lay the child on her back, please," Marie Laveau said as she sat beside Mama Maybelle on the black leather couch.

Maybelle laid Margaret's limp body on the floor and gently brushed the girl's disheveled hair from her forehead.

Marie Laveau thrust the hen's head between her toes and squeezed the fowl's neck with the thin digits.

With a sharp yank of the hen's legs, the bird's body separated from its head.

Marie Laveau pointed the headless fowl at Margaret's face, painting it red with the hen's blood.

The voodoo queen then drew a crimson cross upon her own forehead and on her left big toe, using the bird's bloody, squirming neck.

A moment later, Marie Laveau sat bolt upright. Her hands convulsed erratically and her eyes rolled around in her head like swirling marbles on an agitated plate. After a short while, her eyes steadied themselves. Madame Laveau perused her surroundings. Her parlor – and Mama Maybelle – was gone, replaced by a forest of red lollipops. She was definitely in the realm of a child's soul.

In the distance, standing in a field of auburn grass, stood a tiny silhouette.

"Margaret," the voodoo queen whispered.

Madame Laveau sauntered toward the distant field, locking her gaze on Margaret's silhouette.

As she neared the field, she paused. "O, Bondye mwen, nou pwal gen yon batay sou men nou!" – *"Oh, my God, we gon' have a fight on our hands!"* The blades of grass were not grass at all, she realized, but were, in fact, a sea of severed fingers pointing skyward.

Margaret's silhouette skipped a few paces toward Madame Laveau and then stopped. The silhouette seemed to fold in upon itself and then unfold, revealing Margaret – now clean and cheerful and innocent. The little girl locked her gaze upon Marie Laveau's face. Smiling, she raised her arms to the height of her shoulders, holding them wide apart, as if she hugged a huge ball.

The field of fingers rose in unison with Margaret's arms, until they hovered around her like a swarm of bumblebees.

Marie Laveau quickly unraveled her head-wrap, allowing her hair to fall to her shoulders. She then began to twirl the head-wrap, drawing a big circle in the air before her.

Margaret slammed her hands together. The fingers rocketed toward Marie Laveau like bullets shot from a Sharps carbine.

The old sorceress twirled the head-wrap at a breakneck pace. The spinning cloth emitted a brilliant white light, which took the shape of a round shield, behind which Madame Laveau crouched.

The finger-projectiles struck the shield of light en masse, making a sound akin to torrential rain beating down upon a tin roof.

As the fingers struck the shield, they disintegrated, leaving whiffs of white smoke in their wake.

The air reeked of charred flesh and syrupy sweet confections.

Madame Laveau ceased twirling her head-wrap. The shield of light dissipated. She then tossed the center of the head-wrap over her head, covering her face and neck and wrapped the rest around her wrists and her waist.

The white light returned, erupting from Madame Laveau's pores. A second later, she had transformed into a being of pure light.

Margaret's mouth opened wide and a thunderous peal erupted from it. A viscous, brown fog – accompanied by the stench of human feculence and spoiled milk – billowed from the girl's gaping maw.

Marie Laveau's light form charged forward, closing quickly on the malodorous fog. She thrust the palm of her right hand forward and a column of light erupted from it. The light cut into the sticky fog, cleaving it nearly in half.

The fog dissipated.

Madame Laveau continued to press forward, battering Margaret with a volley of light.

Margaret was knocked off her feet, landing hard on her back with a loud thump.

Madame Laveau's light form leapt toward Margaret, continuing to pummel her with beams of light.

Marie Laveau's right foot slammed down onto Margaret's chest.

Margaret opened her mouth to scream, but the din was beat back by a column of light, which Madame Laveau shot into the girl's mouth.

Margaret convulsed violently. Light spilled from her ears; her nostrils; and the corners of her eyes.

A moment later, Margaret was consumed in light. A second after that, her world of lollipop forests and finger fields were similarly consumed.

Marie Laveau collapsed.

Mama Maybelle caught the old sorceress in one of her massive arms.

Madame Laveau's eyes fluttered open and she smiled. "She clean now, mere."

Mama Maybelle helped Madame Laveau stand as she cast a glance at Margaret, who now slept peacefully on the floor. "Thank you."

Marie Laveau fixed her skirt, wiping the wrinkles out of it with the back of her hand. She pulled loose strands of hair from her face before turning away from Mama Maybelle and walking toward the staircase. "Bring Margaret upstairs to the first room on the left. She'll need a day or so to recover and I'll have to give her a readin' when she wake up."

"Alright, child," Mama Maybelle replied.

"Now, I'm goin' to bed," Marie Laveau said. "Legba say an old suitor is comin' and I need my beauty sleep."

CHAPTER 55

May 9, 1865

Harriet leapt from *The Nefertiti*, landing in her front yard amongst the carnage left by the Union Army and Caleb's army of ghuls. "Lawd!"

Harriet ran toward her house, leaping onto the porch in one bound. She kicked the door open and charged inside the house. "Mama! Daddy!"

"We here, baby," she heard her mother whisper.

Harriet darted into the kitchen toward her mother's voice.

Papa Ben crept out of the cupboard; Mama Rit followed closely behind him, her hands clutching her husband's waist.

Harriet embraced them both. "Thank the Lawd y'all alright! What happened here?"

"The Sec'tary o' war come back here with a bunch o' Blue Coats to kill that cowboy out there on the front lawn and his army o' demons," Papa Ben said.

"Edwin Stanton came *back* here?" Harriet inquired. "He came here lookin' for me before, huh?"

"Yep," Papa Ben replied. "He came here the first time with his hunters lookin' for you. This time, just him and that giant of a woman showed up with all them soldiers. They said they'd kill us if we didn't help them get that cowboy."

"Which way did Stanton and the big woman go?" Harriet asked.

"I reckon he went straight to Hell," Mama Rit answered.

"Stanton's dead?" Harriet asked.

"Yep," Mama Rit replied. "The cowboy killed him."

"You mean the cowboy stain in the front yard?"

"That's Black Mary Fields," Harriet said to her parents without looking Mary's way.

Mary nodded toward Harriet's parents. "I would hug you both, but I got dead man on my hands." She nudged Harriet with her elbow. "Enjoy your folks," she whispered. "Me and Baas gon' clean up out there."

"Thank you," Harriet whispered.

Harriet returned her attention to her parents. "Well, I think y'all safe now," Harriet said. "I have to head out in a couple of hours, but I figure we can..."

Harriet's world somersaulted, carrying her – like a great ship – from a shore of consciousness to a sea of darkness.

The darkness gave way to a vast desert. A few yards ahead of Harriet, the sand began to swirl in a violent spiral. A moment later, the sand erupted, spewing into the air like a geyser.

Out of this fount strolled John Brown; Caleb's coachman's hat sat tilted upon his head. His shirt flew open, revealing a single, blue eye in the center of his chest and a drooling, twisted mouth just above his navel.

The John Brown ghul raised its hands above its head and out of the ground arose a legion of naked toddlers with coal-black skin. John Brown and the toddlers charged toward Harriet...and then the sea of darkness dried and she found herself, once again, on the shore of sentience.

Papa Ben cradled Harriet's head in her arms as he sat beside her on the floor.

"Lawd, no," Harriet gasped, leaping to her feet. Lock the door behind me!"

"Baby, what's wrong?" Mama Rit asked.

"*Everything*, Mama," Harriet replied. "It's *all* wrong."

Harriet drew the *Bello Mule* from its holster and sprinted out the front door. She leapt from the porch, landing near Baas and

Black Mary, who were busily scraping up the remains of ghuls with shovels.

"Where is Pasteur's body?" Harriet asked.

"What's going on, Harriet?" Baas inquired.

"No time, Baas," Harriet replied. "Pasteur's body…where?"

"He's on that heap with all those other unlucky bastards," Mary said, pointing toward a mound of ensanguined body parts that lay in the fire pit.

Harriet sprinted to the fire pit. She rummaged through the carnage until she was covered in rank, greenish-black gore. "He ain't here!"

"Who ain't?" Mary asked, jogging toward the fire pit.

"Pasteur…John Brown," Harriet replied. "The cowboy gone too."

"What?" Baas gasped, running to Harriet's side. "How?"

"The Lawd showed me," Harriet replied. "John Brown and that cowboy from Hell…they one now."

"Well, he couldn't have gone *too* far," Black Mary said, cracking her knuckles. "Baas, pull some kinda magnify-findem-ometer goggles doo-dad outta your bag of tricks and let's hunt him down!"

"If only I had such an invention," Baas sighed. "Much obliged for the idea, though. And what of your senses, Mary? Are you picking up anything?"

"Well, he smells like all the other death 'round here; as far as hearing him, he must have scurried off when I was in the house makin' the acquaintance of Ma and Pa Tubman."

"Ross," Harriet said.

"What?" Mary inquired.

"Their names are Ben and Rit Ross," Harriet replied.

"Mary scratched her head and craned her neck toward Harriet. "And *Tubman* is?"

"My married name," Harriet said. "Long story."

"I swear, this gets better and better," Black Mary chuckled. "You…married; you and Baas; Baas and Marie Laveau…"

"So," Baas chimed in, interrupting Mary's fun. "Are we going after John Brown or are we continuing on our mission to retrieve Ben?"

"Ben," Harriet replied. "I reckon John Brown will be coming after *us*."

CHAPTER 56

May 9, 1865

Harriet, Baas Bello and Black Mary sat in a carriage, staring at a large corner house across the street, on the 1900 block of North Rampart Street in New Orleans.

Black Mary closed her eyes and inhaled deeply. "She's serving coffee and them little fried cakes…the ones with the powdered sugar on 'em."

"Beignets," Baas whispered.

"Umm…yeah; what *he* said," Black Mary said. "I'm hearin' three voices – two old women and a little girl and…wait…somebody just farted upstairs."

"Ben?" Harriet inquired.

"Don't rightly know," Mary replied. "If it is him, that boy needs to lay off the beans; damn!"

"Baas and me will talk to Marie Laveau," Harriet said. "Maybe we can convince her to give Ben up without a fight. I don't want those civilians gettin' hurt. Mary, please…don't rattle no cages."

"I won't start nothin," Mary said. "But, about them civilians…the little girl just called one of them women *Mama Maybelle*."

"Lawd," Harriet sighed.

"Why so glum?" Black Mary asked, smiling. "I've been *waitin'* to throw hands with that old buffalo."

"Apparently, the feeling is mutual," Baas said, pointing toward Marie Laveau's house.

Standing on the porch, with her gaze locked on Black Mary and a broad smile spread across her plump face, was Mama Maybelle.

"Come on, y'all," Mary said, leaping from the carriage. "Let's say hello."

"We just want the boy," Harriet called to Mama Maybelle as she climbed out of the carriage.

And you'll have him, child," Mama Maybelle said. "For a fair exchange, that is."

Baas tipped his boiler-man cap. "What does Marie want?"

"Come on in and find out," Mama Maybelle said, stooping down and inching through the doorway sideways.

Harriet, Baas and Mary followed her into the house.

Standing before them, with Ben kneeling beside her like an obedient dog sitting at its master's heels, was Marie Laveau. The sorceress was dressed in a red formal dress with black, lace trim. Her hair was pulled back and tied in a bun. Atop her crown was a miniscule, red top-hat with a black band and tiny red feather.

She locked eyes with Baas and smiled. "Baas Bello; you haven't aged a day!"

"You, on the other hand, have aged many," Baas said.

Madame Laveau pouted. "Now Baas, play nice, or I might just have to kill your little girlfriends."

"Ah, I see why you left the old hag now, Baas," Black Mary said. She mean as a tiger with a toothache."

"You ain't *seen* mean, cher," Madame Laveau said, leering at Black Mary. "But keep talkin' and you will."

"We didn't come to start any trouble," Harriet said. We just come for my nephew, Ben."

"You started trouble when you stole my husband!" Madame Laveau spat.

"You don't have to *steal* an apple when it *jump* in your basket," Harriet replied.

"The only way you get to leave here with the boy is if Baas drinks this," Marie Laveau hissed, pulling a glass tube, filled with a fluorescent liquid, from between her breasts.

"What is that?" Baas asked.

"Absinthe; puffer fish; giant cane toad; and a few other…things," Marie Laveau answered. She thrust the tube toward her ex-husband. "Drink it, Baas. Drink it and be mine again; don't and the boy stays."

"That concoction will cause permanent brain damage," Baas said. "I will be of no use to you."

"You won't be smart no more, cher," Madame Laveau said. "But you'll be *sweet*; that's what matters most."

"Lady, you'd better get to lookin'," Mary began. "'cause you done lost your mind!"

Marie Laveau's face twisted into a scowl. "I done had enough of you!"

Thunder exploded just outside the house, shaking the parlor.

Harriet's hand crept toward the *Bello Mule*.

A second crack of thunder rent the air.

Marie Laveau staggered backward, clutching her belly. Blood poured from between her fingers.

Harriet pulled Ben to his feet as she drew the *Bello Mule*. She perused the room.

Baas and Black Mary had taken cover behind the parlor's eastern wall. Marie Laveau had collapsed onto her back. Her back arched violently upward as she struggled for breath. Mama Maybelle had bounded up the stairs, disappearing into one of the rooms.

A window in the parlor was shattered and glass covered the floor.

John Brown's bearded face – the true face of the madman – peeked through the window. "Here's Johnny!"

John Brown chuckled. "I like that. One day, I will be heralded in that manner."

Harriet fired *The Mule*.

John Brown's face bifurcated, forming a fork, like the tongue of a rattlesnake. A moment later, his head reformed, the flesh stitching itself back together.

"Ouch," John Brown said, rubbing his forehead. "I imagine I'd be dead if my brain was still in my head."

'I imagine so," Harriet said.

"John Brown climbed through the window frame. "Madame Laveau isn't dead yet, is she? If not, after I infect her, she'll heal right up. I think I'll make her my bride."

"Too late," Harriet said. "You killed her."

"Oh, well," John Brown said, shrugging his shoulders. "Well, ladies…any takers?

"I am going to take your head off your shoulders if you don't tell me where my grandbaby is right now!" Mama Maybelle shouted from the balcony.

"She's safe," John Brown said. "I can't have you taking revenge for the death of your son, now can I?"

"That doesn't concern you, child," Mama Maybelle replied.

John Brown ripped his shirt open. The wooden buttons flew all over the parlor. "I beg to differ." Etched into John Brown's chest was Caleb's face. The face flashed Mama Maybelle a broad grin.

"Give me my granddaughter, child, and I promise I won't come after you," Mama Maybelle said.

"Once I am a safe distance from here, I will send word of Margaret's whereabouts," John Brown said. "I don't want to harm any of you…yet. I am more concerned with building my army."

"I'm concerned with killin' you again and seein' that you *stay* dead this time," Black Mary said, stepping out from behind the wall.

"Mama Maybelle," John Brown crooned. "If you kill this woman, I will bring Margaret to you within the quarter hour."

"Go fetch her then, child," Mama Maybelle said as she descended the stairs. "By the time you return, Black Mary Fields will be dead."

"See you soon," John Brown said, turning toward the window frame. He leapt through it, disappearing amongst the shadows.

"I'm sorry, child," Mama Maybelle said. "But Margaret is more important to me than *any*one's life."

"No need to apologize," Mary said, sauntering toward the door. "I just hope that '*any*one' you talkin' 'bout includes your own life, 'cause you're about to lose it."

Mama Maybelle's beefy fist slammed into Black Mary's chest.

Mary was sent flying backward. Her back crashed into the front door and then it – and Black Mary – tumbled out onto the front lawn.

Mama Maybelle charged through the doorway. Black Mary stood defiantly before her. The heavy mahogany door rested at Mary's feet.

Black Mary kicked the door, sending it speeding toward Mama Maybelle's head. She took off behind it, drawing her revolvers. She fired two shots from both guns and then holstered them as she continued to run toward the giantess.

Mama Maybelle turned her shoulder toward the torpedoing door. It shattered upon impact with the giantess' thick body, sending slivers of wood billowing into the air.

A bullet struck Mama Maybelle's right brow, shattering it. Shards of bone riddled her right eye, sending the giantess reeling in pain.

Black Mary closed on Mama Maybelle, pounding her fists into the colossus' jaw, temples and ribs in a lightning-quick combination.

Mama Maybelle collapsed onto one knee.

Black Mary exploded upward with her knee toward Mama Maybelle's chin.

Fighting through the searing pain in her head, Mama Maybelle blocked the knee strike with a downward elbow strike to Black Mary's thigh.

Mary let loose an agonized yelp as her femur turned to dust beneath the crushing force of Mama Maybelle's strike combined with the tremendous power of her own knee strike.

Black Mary fell onto her chest.

Mama Maybelle raised her massive fists above her head. "Bye, child." She brought down her fists with a fearsome power.

The giantess' fists beat a crater into the earth as they struck the soil. Black Mary was gone. "What? Where is she?"

Maybelle looked around, struggling to focus with her one functioning eye. Baas came into view as Harriet's illusion faded. He was dragging Mary toward the carriage…and standing before her, with the *Bello Mule* pointed at her head, was Harriet.

Mama Maybelle exploded into the air, her powerful legs launching her in a high arch above Harriet's head.

Harriet leapt backward, firing a volley of bullets skyward.

A round struck Mama Maybelle in the chest; another struck her neck and a third speared through her functioning eye. The eye disintegrated, leaving nothing but a moist socket in the giantess' skull.

Blinded, Mama Maybelle plummeted to the earth, landing with a sickening crunch as her skull struck the cobblestone street. A stream of gun-smoke billowed from Mama Maybelle's empty eye sockets.

"Is she dead?" Black Mary asked, pulling herself into the carriage.

"Probably not," Baas replied.

Black Mary sat across from Ben, who was now sleeping, with his head pressed against the side of the carriage. His lips were curled upward in a peaceful smile.

"Damn, I wish I had some of what you been takin'," Mary groaned.

Baas climbed into the driver's seat. Harriet leapt up onto the carriage and took a seat next to Baas.

Baas snapped the reins and the horses took off, pulling the carriage along with them. "When we get to *The Nefertiti*, we have to treat Mary quickly."

"I know; her leg looks bad," Harriet sighed.

"With such extensive damage to her leg, she'll have to lose it, or bleed to death when the femoral artery inevitably ruptures," Baas said. "If she wasn't Gifted, she'd already be dead."

"Umm…y'all *do* know I can hear y'all?" Black Mary shouted.

"Apologies," Baas replied. "Just rest assured that we will have you back to raising perdition in no time."

"Good," Mary said. "Then, me and that mountain of a woman can have our rematch!"

Harriet shot a glance at Baas and shook her head. "Lawd."

CHAPTER 57

May 12, 1865

Baas sat back in a chair, savoring his hot mug of heavily sweetened and creamed coffee. Harriet stepped out of the kitchen carrying two plates atop which sat a piece of blackberry cobbler.

"You're spoiling me," Baas said, taking the plate of cobbler that Harriet offered to him. "One more day of this and you won't be able to get rid of me."

"Sorry to disappoint you, Baas, but if I'm the reason you're stayin', well, I'm all better now."

Harriet turned toward the voice. Mary descended the stairs slowly. She was dressed in a golden-yellow, silk kimono – a gift from Baas.

"How is the leg?" Baas inquired.

Mary pulled up the bottom of the kimono to mid-thigh, exposing her mechanical right leg.

The leg, composed mainly of brass components, was driven by an intricate system of copper gears, pistons and pulleys, all powered by a miniscule steam engine.

"Works like a charm," Mary replied. She jogged and skipped around the living room, showing off her skill with the prosthetic. "See!"

"Good," Baas said. "Very good!"

"So, what's the gospel on John Brown?" Black Mary asked.

"No trace of him yet," Harriet replied.

"And Ben?" Mary asked.

"He's slowly, but surely shakin' off the effects of whatever Marie Laveau poisoned him with," Harriet answered. "He's back with his mother now."

"So, what are we doing now?" Mary asked.

“Waiting,” Harriet answered.

“On?” Mary inquired.

“On the Lawd to show me a sign,” Harriet replied. “It won’t be long, just be ready when He do.”

Mary leaned toward Harriet as if they were sharing some great secret. “Ready for what?”

Harriet felt the world tilt ever so slightly. “War.”

Made in United States
Troutdale, OR
01/14/2024

16934300R00097